Also by **Barbara O'Connor**

Beethoven in Paradise
Me and Rupert Goody
Moonpie and Ivy
Fame and Glory in Freedom, Georgia

TAKING CARE OF MOSES

BARBARA O'CONNOR

TAKING CARE of MOSES

FRANCES FOSTER BOOKS
Farrar, Straus and Giroux
New York

www.fsgkidsbooks.com

Library of Congress Cataloging-in-Publication Data
O'Connor, Barbara.
    Taking care of Moses / Barbara O'Connor.— 1st ed.
        p.   cm.
    Summary: When dissension erupts in the town of Foley, South Carolina,
after a baby is left on the steps of the Rock of Ages Baptist Church, eleven-year-
old Randall must decide whether or not to keep secret his knowledge of who
the foundling's mother is.
    ISBN 0-374-38038-4
    [1. Secrets—Fiction.   2. Conduct of life—Fiction.   3. Foundlings—
Fiction.   4. Interpersonal relations—Fiction.   5. Church—Fiction.   6. South
Carolina—Fiction.]   I. Title.

PZ7.O217Tak 2004
[Fic]—dc22

                                                                2003049466

For Janet Zade
with thanks for all you do
and all you are

TAKING CARE OF MOSES

1

Randall Mackey had a secret. He knew who left the baby in the cardboard box on the front steps of the Rock of Ages Baptist Church.

He worried and worried about the secret, not knowing whether or not he should tell someone. But Randall was afraid that if he told even one person, something bad might happen to Queenie.

His worry felt like a hot, heavy blanket, covering him from head to toe. After worrying for three days, Randall decided the answer was no. He wouldn't tell anyone. Not even Jaybird.

"What's wrong with you, anyway?" Jaybird said, poking Randall with his pointy elbow.

"Nothing," Randall said, hoping Jaybird couldn't see the worry that was jumping around inside him.

"Then how come you acting so weird?"

"I'm not acting weird."

"Yeah, you are, too."

Randall dropped three peanuts into his soda bottle. Plunk, plunk, plunk, fizz.

Randall and Jaybird sat on a tattered blue tarp under Jaybird's front porch. It was cool and damp under there. They could look out at the world through the spaces in the crisscrossed wood of the rotting lattice that surrounded the porch. They could see who came and went at Jaybird's house. Could identify them by their shoes, going up or down the steps.

When they saw Althea's plaid sneakers stop at the bottom of the steps, they sat as still as statues, not making a sound.

"Preacher Ron said that baby has the grippe," Althea called out into the air.

Randall and Jaybird sat frozen, grinning at each other. Blinking. Quiet.

Althea's face appeared outside the latticework. She peered into the darkness under the porch.

"I *said*, Preacher Ron said that baby has the grippe," she hollered.

"What's 'the grippe'?" Randall asked, ignoring Jaybird's elbow jab. Randall and Jaybird had made a pact never to speak one word to Althea again. But Randall couldn't help it. He wanted to know about the baby.

"How should I know?" Althea said. She stuck her chewing gum under the steps and skipped down the crumbling sidewalk toward the street. But then she stopped. She came back over to the porch and squatted down, peering through the lattice again. "That baby has a hammertoe, too," she said.

Jaybird crawled over to the lattice. "You don't know nothing about nothing," he said. "Get your ugly self out of here before I'm forced to spit on you again."

Althea stood up and jabbed the toe of her shoe into the red dirt, sending dust and gravel spewing into the fort.

"And that baby's got scaly worm," she said.

Randall crawled over to the lattice and tried to see Althea's face. All he could see was her skinny brown legs. "Did Preacher Ron say that?" he asked.

"Maybe." Then Althea skipped off down the sidewalk and out of sight.

"She lies bigger than anything," Jaybird said, still peering out through the lattice. Then he whirled around to face Randall. "I thought we wasn't gonna talk to her no more," he said.

Randall didn't answer. He stretched out on the blue tarp and looked up at the wooden boards of the porch above them. Sometimes Althea dropped things through the cracks. Raisins or gum wrappers or chicken bones. Once she poured cherry Kool-Aid down on their heads, making Jaybird scurry out from under the porch and pinch her. Hard.

Randall Mackey was grateful for Jaybird Gilley. All of Randall's other friends had moved away, one by one. And each time one family moved out, a black family moved in. Before long, the Mackeys were the only white family left on Woodmont Street. Randall had needed to make a new friend, but it seemed like the black kids who moved into his old friends' houses weren't much interested in him.

But Jaybird was different. The very first day the Gilleys moved in, Jaybird had spotted Randall and had hollered, "I got a secret fort. You wanna see it?"

Randall had dashed across the street and crawled up under the porch with Jaybird. They had scooped the damp earth with their hands to make a comfortable place to sit. Then they had watched Jaybird's aunts and uncles and cousins and stepbrothers carry furniture and boxes up the steps and into the house. Jaybird had put a name to each and every pair of shoes. Cousin Eula Mae in the blue flip-flops. Uncle Irving in the dirty work boots. Stepbrother Curtis in the high-top sneakers.

Randall had never seen so many people in one family. He hadn't had that much fun in a long time. But best of all, he had watched Jaybird's little sister, Althea, try and try to join them in their fort under the porch. But no sooner had she poked one leg up under there than Jaybird smacked her with a yardstick. Hard.

Althea had yanked her leg back and hollered, "Dang, doggit, you, Jaybird. I'm tellin'!"

"No you ain't, you little she-devil," Jaybird had called out through the lattice. " 'Cause you're a chick, chick, chicken."

Then that leg of hers had started kicking at them so fast Jaybird couldn't even hit it with the yardstick.

Randall had never heard kids talk as peculiar as Jaybird and Althea. And he had never seen such hitting and kicking. He was delighted. Randall didn't have a brother or sister. He could only dream about smacking someone's leg with a yardstick.

Now their fort under the Gilleys' porch was all fixed up with a blue tarp, an assortment of supplies (like playing cards and saltine crackers), and a shoebox full of gravel for hurling at Althea.

"You think that baby really has a hammertoe?" Randall said.

Jaybird shook his head. "Naw."

"Maybe that's why that baby got left there for Preacher Ron to find," Randall said. " 'Cause he's got so many things wrong with him that couldn't even his mama fix him."

"Naw," Jaybird said. "That don't sound right."

"Why else would someone leave a baby like that?"

Jaybird shrugged. "Just didn't want him, I reckon." He tossed his soda bottle into the plastic milk crate he and Randall used to haul stuff to the fort. "I wonder who left that baby, anyway," he said.

Randall's stomach clumped up into a knot. He kept his face away from Jaybird and dug his feet into the cool, damp dirt along the edge of the house.

Randall Mackey had a secret. He knew who left the baby in the cardboard box on the front steps of the Rock of Ages Baptist Church.

2

Randall had thought about telling his secret to Mr. Avery, but then he decided not to. He figured Mr. Avery probably had enough stuff to worry about now that his wife, Queenie, was acting so peculiar.

Mr. Avery was the custodian at Thomas and Sons Insurance Agency where Randall's father worked. Ever since Randall was little, Queenie had loved his drawings. She taped them on the walls of the Averys' tiny apartment in the basement of the insurance agency. She taped them on the cupboards and doors and windows. She always told Randall he had a gift.

"You got a real gift, Randall," she'd say. "And you know what? Can't nobody take your gift away from you. That's the best kind, isn't it?"

Randall would smile and blush and feel good about himself and his gift.

But then something strange started happening to

Queenie. Sometimes when Randall came to visit, she called him Monroe.

Randall would say, "You mean Randall."

At first Queenie would say, "Randall. Yes, that's what I mean. Randall."

But after a while, when he said, "You mean Randall," Queenie would cock her head and squint at him. She'd grin and say, "You're just teasin' me, right, Monroe?"

Mr. Avery told Randall that Monroe was Queenie's brother, who had died twenty years ago.

Then one day Queenie went to the beauty parlor in her nightgown. Agnes Worthy had phoned Mr. Avery to come and get her because she was talking crazy and hollering at all the ladies sitting under the hair dryers. Agnes told Randall's mother that Queenie had been drunk.

But Randall's mother said, "Why, I've never known Queenie Avery to touch a drop of liquor in her life." She shook her head and said, "Isn't that strange?"

Then things got worse. Queenie ate cat food. Queenie used swear words in church. Queenie wouldn't change her clothes. Not even to sleep. And then Queenie started wandering. Right out the back door of Thomas and Sons Insurance Agency and clear on down the street until Mr. Avery went running after her and brought her home again.

Queenie would look at Mr. Avery with wide, surprised eyes and say, "Well, hello, mister." That's what she called him. Mister. Long after she stopped knowing who anybody was anymore—even folks she'd known her whole life—she knew Mr. Avery. And she always called him mister.

After a while, folks started telling Mr. Avery that Queenie shouldn't stay in the basement apartment with him anymore. They said Queenie belonged in a special place where she could get the care she needed.

Whenever anybody said that, Mr. Avery got mad. "I can take care of Queenie. We been taking care of each other for forty-seven years."

The ladies from the Rock of Ages Baptist Church would sit on Mr. Avery's tattered sofa, sipping iced tea and talking in soft voices.

"But, Felton," they'd say, "Queenie's in a bad way. She might wander off and get lost or hurt. You wouldn't want that, now, would you?"

But Mr. Avery wouldn't listen. So folks took turns staying with Queenie while Mr. Avery worked upstairs in the insurance agency. And every Sunday someone stayed with her so Mr. Avery could go to church.

But more and more, folks wagged their heads and muttered about poor old Mr. Avery and pitiful little Queenie and how something really needed to be done. They told Mr. Avery that if Queenie kept wandering off like that, he was going to have to send her away to a special home so she would be safe.

Randall felt bad for Mr. Avery. He wished he could do something to make him feel better. So he kept bringing his drawings over to their basement apartment, even though Queenie called him Monroe all the time now. Sometimes Mr. Avery looked really sad, and once he said to Randall, "If my Queenie gets sent away, I might as well lay down and die."

So when Randall had seen Queenie shuffling up Woodmont Street in the dark, he got scared. He didn't know what to do. He was supposed to go straight home from Jaybird's house after supper. Jaybird's mama had called Randall's house and said he was on his way home. Randall had seen the front porch light flick on at his house. He knew his mama was waiting. She would be spitting mad if he didn't come home right away.

"Queenie," Randall had called out in a loud whisper.

But Queenie had kept on walking, right up the middle of the street, clutching her big red purse. Her thin nightgown clung to her bony legs. She wore high-heeled shoes that flopped on her feet and made scuffling noises on the asphalt street.

She turned the corner at Randall's house and kept walking toward town. Randall stopped at the corner. He looked at his house, then he looked at Queenie, getting farther and farther away. His thoughts were yanking him back and forth. Home. Queenie. Home. Queenie.

Randall raced up the street after Queenie. She had turned onto Cold Creek Road, heading toward the church. The sound of her scuffling high heels echoed in the still night air. By the time Randall caught up with her, she had stopped to watch moths fluttering around the dim streetlight. Randall started to say something, but a noise made him and Queenie both look over at the church. And that's when Randall saw who left the baby in the cardboard box on the front steps of the Rock of Ages Baptist Church.

Of course, he didn't *know* there was a baby in the box. The person who left the box didn't look at Randall or Queenie. The person just set the box down and ran away, disappearing into the night.

Before Randall could get his head to settle down and think about what was going on, he heard footsteps on the sidewalk behind him. He turned to see a flashlight bobbing in the darkness toward him.

"Queenie?" Mr. Avery called out in a trembling voice.

Queenie smiled and said, "Hello, mister."

Mr. Avery draped his ratty old sweater over her shoulders and said, "Come on home now, Queenie."

And then he saw Randall. His whole face dropped down so droopy and sad that Randall felt a stab inside himself.

"Hey, Randall," Mr. Avery said. "I didn't expect to see you out here so late."

"I ate supper at Jaybird's," Randall said.

"Oh."

Mr. Avery and Randall looked down at their feet. Queenie started humming.

"Queenie was looking for that mangy old cat that's been hanging around our place," Mr. Avery said.

"Oh," Randall said.

If a lie could come alive, like a living, breathing thing, Mr. Avery's lie would have danced all around them out there under the stars in the middle of the street.

And when Randall looked at Mr. Avery's face in the shadowy glow of the streetlight, he could see all the words that Mr. Avery didn't say. "Please don't tell anyone you saw Queenie wandering out here like this," his face said. "They want to send Queenie away," it said. "But I need her to stay with me."

And Randall hoped that his own face showed the words that he didn't say: "I won't tell anyone that I saw Queenie wandering out here like this."

And then Randall heard his mama calling his name, loud and irritated from his front porch.

So he said goodbye and ran toward home. When he got to the corner, he turned to look back. Mr. Avery and Queenie were walking slowly, arm in arm. The sound of Queenie's humming and scuffling grew fainter and fainter.

Mrs. Mackey had been really mad that Randall hadn't come straight home. He had wanted to borrow Mr. Avery's lie about the cat. "I was looking for a cat," he had wanted to say. But Randall was a terrible liar. So he just said, "Sorry."

He had gone to bed that night thinking about Queenie and knowing for sure he wasn't going to tell anybody that he had seen her wandering in the street in her nightgown.

But the next day, Randall found out something that made his stomach squeeze up into a worry ball. Preacher Ron had found the cardboard box on the front steps of the Rock of Ages Baptist Church. And inside the box was a baby! A squealing, gurgling baby. Tucked inside the box with the baby was a note. "Please take care of me," it read.

And then the whole town of Foley, South Carolina, began to buzz. "Who in the world left that baby?" they buzzed. "Where on earth did this child come from?" they said.

Randall knew right away that he had a problem. If he told anyone that he had seen who left the baby in the cardboard box, wouldn't he have to tell about Queenie, too? Wouldn't somebody say, "What in tarnation were you doing way over at the church at night like that?"

Yes, somebody surely would. And Randall couldn't tell the truth. If he told the truth, somebody might send Queenie away. And then Mr. Avery would lay down and die.

If he couldn't tell the truth, then he would have to tell a lie. And Randall was a terrible liar. That just left one choice. Randall Mackey would have to keep his secret all to himself.

3

That Sunday Randall sat between his mother and father in the middle of the third row on the right side of the Rock of Ages Baptist Church. He had been coming to this church for eleven years, his whole life, and had never sat anywhere else. One time Jaybird tried to get him to sit with the Gilleys in the sixth row on the left side, but Randall said no.

Randall was glad the Gilleys had decided to join the Rock of Ages Baptist Church. Mrs. Gilley had needed a church that she and Jaybird and Althea could walk to, since she didn't drive and Mr. Gilley wasn't much of a churchgoer. But then she found out that none of the other black folks on Woodmont Street went there. In fact, no other black folks went there at all.

"I don't know, Iris," Mrs. Gilley had said to Randall's mother. "Maybe we should go on over to Southside Baptist where my sister goes."

"Well, that's just plumb crazy, Lottie," Mrs. Mackey had said. "That church is clear over in Duncan Springs. How are y'all gonna get there? Besides, the Rock of Ages Baptist Church prides itself on being 'the little church with the big heart,'" Mrs. Mackey had told her, quoting the sign on the wall behind the organ. "Your family is welcome in our church."

So now every Sunday Mrs. Gilley and Jaybird and Althea sat in the sixth row on the left side of the tiny brick church on Cold Creek Road.

While the offering plate was passed around, Randall glanced back at the Gilleys. Jaybird looked stiff and miserable in his brown suit and green tie, but Althea looked happy as anything. Her braids stuck up every which way and wiggled as she bobbed her head in time to the music. Her fingers played an invisible organ on the back of the pew in front of her.

When Mr. Avery started snoring, Althea clamped her hands over her mouth and glanced gleefully around her to see if anyone else had noticed. If they had, they didn't let on. Most everyone figured Mr. Avery needed some rest after cleaning the insurance agency and taking care of Queenie every day.

"BROTHERS and SISTERS," Preacher Ron shouted, making Randall jump. "I speak to you now of BROTHERLY LOVE." Preacher Ron said the last two words slow and loud, then paused for a long time. The room was quiet except for the soft rustle of paper as folks fanned themselves with their church bulletins.

Randall doodled in a small spiral notebook in his lap. He didn't really listen to Preacher Ron's sermon, but every now and then one of those loud words would bust through and interrupt his doodling. SALVATION. DESPAIR. GLORY. INFANT.

Infant? Randall looked up. Preacher Ron was sweating. He loosened his tie and leaned over the pulpit. "Somewhere in our little town of Foley, South Carolina, lives a troubled soul," he said.

Randall's mother nodded. "That's right," she said softly.

"Somewhere in our little town of Foley, South Carolina," Preacher Ron went on, "lives a troubled soul in NEED of a flock."

Mrs. Mackey nodded bigger. "That's right," she said again.

"And WE are that flock." Preacher Ron banged on the pulpit.

Someone in the back of the church hollered out, "Amen!"

Randall's stomach flipped and flopped while Preacher Ron told the congregation all about the baby in the cardboard box. How the box had been left on the steps of the church. How that was surely a sign that the flock of brothers and sisters of the church must embrace the

19

baby and seek out the troubled soul who had given the baby to them.

Folks called out "Yes, brother," and "Praise be," but Randall sat still and quiet. He watched his mother's hands, folded in her lap. Her fingers were short and plump, white and freckled. Then Randall looked down at his father's feet, planted firmly on the dusty wooden floor. His black shoes were scuffed and worn. He tapped his toe when the Celebration Choir sang "Love Lifted Me."

After the service, Randall waited for Jaybird outside the Fellowship Hall behind the church.

Jaybird limped toward Randall. "I don't care what Mama says," he said, "I'm taking these dang shoes off." He untied his shiny brown oxfords and yanked them off.

"I'm tellin'," Althea sang out as she skipped up the sidewalk toward them.

"Like I care, you creeping crud ball." Jaybird wiggled his toes inside his socks. His skinny ankles stuck out from beneath the cuffs of his trousers.

Althea stuck her chin in the air. "I'm going in to see the baby 'cause Mrs. Jennings said I could baby-sit."

"Babies can't baby-sit babies," Jaybird said. "Right, Randall?"

Althea turned her cool gaze to Randall.

"Right," he said, bracing for whatever pain Althea was about to inflict on him.

She stomped the heel of her patent leather shoe on his foot. Then she skipped off down the sidewalk and into the Fellowship Hall.

Randall and Jaybird followed her into the cinder block building. Inside, it was hot and noisy and smelled like coffee and after-shave. Grownups stood in clusters or sat on folding metal chairs and talked while kids darted in and out, snatching brownies and pound cake from the tables that lined the walls.

Randall followed Jaybird through the crowd to where a group of women huddled. Right in the middle of the huddle sat Althea, holding a tiny baby.

"Look," she said, pushing back the pale yellow blanket to reveal the dark brown face of the sleeping baby. "His name is Moses. Ain't that perfect?" she said. "Like in the bulrushes and all?"

"Says who?" Jaybird snapped.

"Says me," a voice behind them said.

Randall and Jaybird looked up at the smiling face of Mrs. Charlotte Jennings, the preacher's wife.

"A baby's got to have a name, right, boys?" she said.

Althea rocked the baby back and forth. Her petticoat made a swish-swish noise against the metal chair.

"What are you going to do with it?" Jaybird asked.

"*Him*," Mrs. Jennings said. "The baby is a *him*. And I'm going to swaddle him in the brotherly love of the church until such time as the troubled soul who has forsaken him comes forward to reclaim him. Like a lost LAMB, he has come to us."

Jaybird looked at Randall and Randall looked at Jaybird. Mrs. Jennings was as good at preaching as her husband, sprinkling her conversation with those loud words like that.

"How are you going to find the troubled soul?" Jaybird asked.

Randall's heart beat fast inside his stiff Sunday shirt. He wondered if his secret showed on his face because the voice inside his head kept hollering, "*I* know who the troubled soul is."

Mrs. Jennings smiled down at the baby in Althea's lap. "We will BIDE our time and hope that LOVE shows the way," she said.

Randall tugged on the sleeve of Jaybird's jacket. "Let's go get some pound cake," he said.

That night, Randall tore a page out of his sketchbook, crumpled it into a ball, and tossed it into his wastebasket. Babies were hard to draw. Randall could draw just about anything. But babies were hard to draw.

Instead of a baby, Randall drew a wagon. Then he drew a cardboard box inside the wagon. Then he drew a tall woman with wild black hair looking into the box. He tried to draw a floppy straw hat on her head, but it looked funny. He erased so much the picture was beginning to smudge. Instead of a hat, Randall put a bow in her wild black hair. He carefully tore the page out of his sketchbook. Usually he saved his drawings for Mr. Avery and Queenie. But not this one. This one he folded into a small square. Then he opened his underwear drawer and pushed the square of folded paper way down under his socks.

He kneeled beside his bed and said his prayers. He ended the same way he always did. "And please watch over . . ." Then he went through his usual list of the people he thought needed to be watched over. (Sometimes Althea was on the list and sometimes she wasn't.) But this time Randall added a new name. Moses.

4

I know somethin' you don't know," Althea sang.

Randall looked at Jaybird.

"Don't pay her no mind," Jaybird said. "She's just trying to get us riled up."

"I know somethin' you don't know," Althea sang again. She waved a garden hose in a figure eight, sending water plopping down onto the porch above Randall and Jaybird. It was so hot out that they didn't mind the cool water dripping through the cracks onto their heads.

"Hey, Althea," Jaybird hollered through the criss-crossed wood of the lattice. "Go tell somebody who gives a hoot."

Althea brought the hose over to the porch and sprayed water onto the ground, turning the red dirt into goopy red mud.

"Okay," she said. "I'll go find somebody who wants

to hear all about how Mrs. Charlotte Jennings and Miss Frieda got into it big time, and Miss Frieda called Mrs. Jennings a nosy do-gooder."

Jaybird held a finger to his lips and said "Shhhhh" to Randall.

"And I bet I know plenty of people who want me to tell them about how Mrs. Jennings said 'Shut up' to Miss Frieda and then she said she was gonna pray for her. Then she had to push Miss Frieda's foot out of the door so she could slam it."

Randall grinned at Jaybird. Jaybird sure was good at tricking Althea into telling stuff.

Althea swished her feet around in the puddle of dirty water beside the porch.

"And I'm gonna make somebody real happy when I tell 'em all about how them two ladies were fighting about Moses," she went on.

Randall scurried out from under the porch.

"Why were they fighting about Moses?" he said.

"I ain't telling you, you dirty rotten nose picker," Althea said. She aimed the hose at Randall's feet, splattering red mud up his legs.

"Come on, Althea," he said. "How come they were fighting about Moses?"

Althea flicked the hose, sending water into the air and then splashing down on Randall's head.

"Who told you that anyway?" Randall said.

Jaybird crawled out from under the porch and tugged on Randall's arm. "Let's go," he said. "She don't know nothing."

"I know Miss Frieda had a hissy fit on Mrs. Jennings's front porch 'cause I saw her," Althea said. "Mama give me some baby clothes to take over there, and I seen everything with my own two eyes, and I heard everything with my own two ears." She kicked water at Jaybird.

"But why were they fighting about Moses?" Randall asked again.

" 'Cause Miss Frieda wants to take him away from Preacher Ron and Mrs. Jennings," Althea said.

"How come?"

Althea shrugged. "Just wants to, I reckon."

"That don't make no sense, Althea," Jaybird said.

"Uh-huh." Althea twirled the hose around in circles, hopping over the water like it was a jump rope. "Miss Frieda says *she's* the foster mama. *She* gets the babies, not Mrs. Jennings."

"Let's go over to Miss Frieda's," Randall said to Jaybird. "Maybe T.J. knows what's going on."

They climbed over the chain link fence behind the Gilleys' house and raced up the alley to Sycamore Road. Miss Frieda lived in a duplex, her on one side and her sister, Earlene, on the other. Jaybird knocked on Miss Frieda's rickety screen door. Inside, a baby was crying. Somebody hollered, "Clean that up off the floor right now, you hear me?"

Two small boys came out of Earlene's side and stared at Jaybird and Randall.

"Is T.J. home?" Jaybird asked.

Just then Miss Frieda's screen door burst open and T.J. ran out.

Someone hollered from inside the house, "Tyrone Jamal, get yourself back in here before I come out there and make you sorry for what you done."

T.J. leaped off the porch, brushing past Randall and Jaybird, and disappeared around the back of the house.

Miss Frieda came out on the porch with a rolled-up magazine clutched in her hand. She shook the magazine in the air and hollered, "This'll be waitin' for you when you get home, boy!"

Jaybird grinned at Randall.

Miss Frieda turned her head real slow and narrowed her fighting-mad eyes at Jaybird.

"What you laughin' at, Jaybird Gilley?" she said.

Jaybird's grin disappeared. In its place he set a look of sweetness and seriousness all mixed together.

"Nothin', Miss Frieda," he said. "We just come over to ask T.J. about Moses."

"Who?"

"Moses."

"Who's Moses?"

"That baby."

"What baby?"

Jaybird poked Randall.

"That baby that was left in the box over at the church," Randall said.

Miss Frieda fanned herself with the magazine. Sweat rolled down the side of her face. She pulled a damp paper towel out of the top of her dress and wiped her neck.

"What you wanna know?" she said. She squeezed her eyes up into a look of suspicion. Randall looked down at his sneakers. He was hoping Jaybird would jump in and take over from there, but he didn't.

"Why do you want to take Moses away from Preacher Ron and Mrs. Jennings?" Randall said, trying hard as anything to make his eyes stop looking at his feet and start looking at Miss Frieda.

Miss Frieda snorted and flapped her hand at Randall.

"Those folks got no business with that baby," she said. "Me and Earlene's the ones to tend to that child. He belongs right in there with all them others." She jerked her head toward the screen door.

A small girl wearing a pink shower cap poked her head out of the door.

"Buddy puked again," she said.

Miss Frieda opened the screen door. "Y'all run on now," she said to Randall and Jaybird. "And if you see T.J., tell him to get hisself on home."

Randall had the sudden urge to follow her inside. He wondered what it would be like to sit on that ratty old couch beside the other kids and watch cartoons and eat graham crackers. He tried to imagine how it would feel if Miss Frieda was his foster mama and called him "baby" and "sugar" and "lamb" like she was always doing to the kids she took in. Randall knew Miss Frieda acted mean sometimes, but mostly she loved all the children who needed her. And he was pretty sure that she had never hit anybody with a rolled-up magazine in her life.

That night after supper, Randall went out on the back porch. He sat in the rusty glider and opened his sketchbook. He used his colored pencils to draw a cardboard box. Then he drew a hand on each side of the box, reaching for the bundled-up baby inside. One hand was white. Underneath that one, Randall wrote, "Mrs. Charlotte Jennings." The other hand was black. Underneath that one, he wrote, "Miss Frieda."

Way up in the corner of the page he drew a big floppy hat. It looked better than the hat he had tried to draw the night before. Randall was pleased that he had finally gotten the hat right. He wished he could show the picture to Mr. Avery and Queenie. But he couldn't. He had made up his mind that he definitely wasn't telling his secret. Not to Mr. Avery. Not to Queenie. Not even to Jaybird. He would put this picture in his sock drawer with the other one.

5

"Ezra, Nehemiah, Esther, Job," Althea sang out. Her jump rope slapped the sidewalk, sending puffs of dirt into the air.

"Althea sure wants to win that Bible drill, huh?" Randall said, peering out through the lattice of the fort.

"She's too dumb," Jaybird said. He scooped peanut butter out of the jar with a cracker.

"Matthew, Mark, Luke, and John;

Acts, Romans, Co-rin-thee-ans."

Althea's sneakers made little squeaky sounds on the sidewalk as she jumped. Slap, squeak, squeak. Slap, squeak, squeak.

Suddenly two legs appeared outside the fort. Randall recognized them. Sunburned. Freckled. Dirty sandals with thick rubber soles.

"Hey, Mom," he called from under the porch.

"Hey, boys." His mother hooked her fingers through

the lattice and squinted into the darkness of the fort. "I need y'all to take some macaroni salad over to Queenie Avery," she said.

Randall and Jaybird crawled out from under the porch. Althea tossed her jump rope into the bushes and ran over.

"Can I go, too?" She grinned up at Mrs. Mackey. A cherry Popsicle had left blotchy red stains down the front of her T-shirt.

"No!" Jaybird said, giving Althea a shove.

"She's going or you ain't," someone called through the screen door.

"Hey, Lottie," Mrs. Mackey called up to Jaybird's mother.

"Hey, Iris," Mrs. Gilley said. "I've got something for Queenie, too. Althea, come in here and get this corn bread."

Althea tossed her head and poked her chin in the air as she stomped past Jaybird and up the front steps.

"Come on in and have some iced tea," Mrs. Gilley called down to Mrs. Mackey.

Randall, Jaybird, and Althea walked down the sidewalk toward Thomas and Sons Insurance Agency. Althea walked with one foot on the curb and the other in the street. Up, down, up, down, she went, calling out books of the Bible with each step.

"Hosea, Amos, Obadiah, Jonah."

"Hush up, ninny brain," Jaybird said. "Nobody wants to hear your nasty self."

"Ephesians, Philippians, Thessalonians," Althea called out even louder.

"You left out Colossians," Randall said.

"Uh-uh."

"Yes you did."

"Did not."

"Althea, you did bigger than anything. You said Philippians and then you said Thessalonians."

"No, I most certainly and definitely did not." Althea stamped her feet as she marched along the curb. Up, down, up, down.

Randall looked at Jaybird, but Jaybird wasn't interested in books of the Bible. He was busy tossing the foil-wrapped corn bread into the air, higher and higher with each toss. Every once in a while, it landed on the sidewalk with a splat.

Randall wished he could just haul off and swat Althea like Jaybird would have. But Randall had never been very good at hitting. He admired the way Jaybird could smack someone so easily and not even feel bad about it.

When they got to Thomas and Sons Insurance Agency, Randall handed the macaroni salad to Althea.

"Wait here," he said.

Sometimes Randall's father got mad when they came to his office. If he wasn't busy, he was happy to see them. He might even let them make paper-clip necklaces or take pictures of their hands on the copy machine. But if he was busy, he got mad. So Randall always went in first to check things out.

When Mr. Mackey saw Randall, he smiled and pushed a stack of papers aside. Randall motioned to Jaybird and Althea through the front door, waving them in.

"Hey there," Mr. Mackey said. "What're y'all up to?" He brushed crumbs off his lap and stood up. His stomach bulged over his belt and his shirt gaped open where a button had popped off.

"We've got stuff for Queenie," Althea said, holding up the macaroni salad.

"Oh, yeah?" Mr. Mackey nodded toward the slightly flattened foil-wrapped package in Jaybird's hand. "Is that your mama's corn bread?"

"Yessir," Althea said. "Want some?"

Jaybird gave her a look, but she yanked the package from him and handed it to Mr. Mackey.

"Have some," she said. "Queenie won't care. She don't eat nothing anyway."

Mr. Mackey chuckled. "Naw, I can't take Queenie's corn bread."

"We're going downstairs," Randall said. Jaybird and Althea followed him along the dark hallway to the back of the office. They had to wind their way through a maze of boxes and file cabinets. A rusty fan, a soda machine, some dead houseplants, a bicycle. A cat darted in front of them and disappeared behind a pile of dusty books.

They made their way down the dimly lit stairs to the basement. The walls were covered with Thomas and Sons calendars. Every single year since 1962.

Randall knocked on Mr. Avery's door. Althea hummed while they waited, and Jaybird said, "Shhhh!"

When Mr. Avery opened the door, the smell of onions drifted into the hall.

"Hey there," Mr. Avery said, wiping his hands on a dish towel.

"We brought some stuff for Queenie," Randall said.

Mr. Avery's long, droopy face lifted into a smile. His thin gray hair hung in greasy clumps down the back of his neck. A stubble of white whiskers covered his chin.

"Come on in," he said, stepping back to let them in.

Althea pranced into the tiny room and plopped down on the couch, cradling the bowl of macaroni salad in her lap.

"It stinks in here," she said.

Mr. Avery laughed. "That dern little ole window won't stay open."

They all looked at the only window in the room, way up toward the ceiling. Long, narrow, and dark with sooty dust.

Mr. Avery went over to the grease-splattered stove in the corner of the room and stirred something in a pan. The door to the bedroom was only open a crack.

Randall heard Queenie's soft snoring. Lately, she slept a lot during the day. Sometimes she slept sitting right there in the kitchen, her head resting on the table beside a bowl of soggy cereal.

Randall reached in his pocket and brought out a folded piece of paper.

"I brought this," he said.

Mr. Avery unfolded the paper and inspected the drawing. "Downy woodpecker, right?"

"Right."

Birds were Randall's specialty, and Mr. Avery knew a lot about birds. Randall always wondered how he knew so much about birds when the only thing he could see from his basement window was the sidewalk above. Sometimes the legs of folks walking by. A dog or two once in a while. But hardly ever a bird.

Mr. Avery smoothed the drawing out on the coffee table. "That's real good, Randall," he said. "I'll show Queenie when she wakes up, okay?"

"Okay." Randall stood up. "We better go."

"I don't have to go," Althea said. "I can sing to Queenie."

"You can't, neither," Jaybird said. He snatched the macaroni salad off Althea's lap and handed it to Mr. Avery.

Althea jumped off the couch and shoved Jaybird with both hands. He grabbed one of her spiky braids and yanked. Randall hurried toward the door.

"Come on, Jaybird," he said. "Bye, Mr. Avery. Tell Queenie we said hey."

*** *** ***

On the way home, Althea rubbed her arm.

"I'm tellin' Mama you knuckle-balled me," she said.

"Go ahead, toad booger," Jaybird said. "Then I'll knuckle-ball your other arm and you can tell again, okay?"

"Hey, look." Randall pointed across the street. "There's Preacher Ron and Moses!"

They raced across the street. Preacher Ron sat on a bench outside Agnes's Cut 'n' Curl beauty parlor, pushing a stroller back and forth with his foot.

"Well, do help us!" he said. "How y'all doin'?"

"Fine," Randall said. "Is that Moses?"

"Yes, it is."

The baby slapped his tiny hands against the front of the stroller and smiled up at them.

"He likes me," Althea said. "Watch this."

She stuck her face down in front of Moses. He squealed and wrapped his chubby fingers around one of Althea's braids.

"See?" Althea beamed up at Preacher Ron.

"When do you think his mama is going to come get him?" Randall said.

"Well now, I can't say." Preacher Ron ran his hand over his smooth, evenly parted hair.

"What if she doesn't ever come back?" Randall said.

Preacher Ron looked down at the baby clutching Althea's braid. Moses made a little noise that sounded like "B-a-a-a-a."

"Well, I reckon we gotta just take this thing one day at a time," he said. "No use in fretting about what-ifs when we got plenty of for-sures to fret about. Right?"

A bell tinkled when the door to the beauty parlor opened, and Mrs. Charlotte Jennings came out. Althea peeled Moses' fingers off her braid and ran over to Mrs. Jennings.

"Can I feel your hair?" Althea said.

Mrs. Jennings looked irritated, but she leaned down to let Althea pat her stiff blond hair.

"This is called a French twist," Althea said to Randall and Jaybird. "Ain't it, Mrs. Jennings?"

"Yes, Althea, it is." Mrs. Jennings fiddled with the pale blue blanket tucked around Moses.

"Is Miss Frieda gonna take Moses to be with her foster kids?" Randall asked.

Mrs. Jennings stood up straight and stiff. "No, Randall," she said. "Moses was delivered to the brothers and sisters of the Rock of Ages Baptist Church. That is the PLAN for Moses. You know about how there is a DIVINE PLAN for each and every one of us, Randall." Mrs. Jennings had slipped into her preaching way of talking, saying particular words real loud so everyone would be sure and get the point.

"But what if the divine plan is for Miss Frieda to take care of Moses until his mama comes back?"

Randall knew he was liable to rile Mrs. Jennings up good, but he just couldn't seem to stop himself.

Mrs. Jennings pursed her lips together tight. Red splotches began to appear on her neck. She glanced at Moses and then said in a low, quiet voice, "But that *isn't* the divine plan, Randall."

"Stop right now," Randall told himself. "Don't you say another word."

But no matter how hard he tried to keep quiet, the words "How do you know?" came out of his mouth.

Mrs. Jennings turned to Preacher Ron. She cocked her head at him and waited.

Preacher Ron cleared his throat. "Well now, Randall, we know—"

"That couldn't be the divine plan," Althea interrupted. " 'Cause Miss Frieda don't go to church. She's a heathen, ain't she, Preacher Ron?" She ran her hand over Moses' fuzzy black hair.

"Besides," she added, "Miss Frieda already has lots of kids and Mrs. Jennings don't have any."

Preacher Ron stood up. "I expect we better get on home now," he said.

Randall watched them push the stroller down the sidewalk and disappear around the corner. His thoughts were so tangled he didn't even answer when Jaybird said, "Let's go look for cans behind the Winn-Dixie." And he didn't pay attention to Althea saying, "Leviticus, Numbers, Deuteronomy."

He looked over at the empty space where, just minutes before, the stroller had been. Then he looked up and caught a glimpse of his reflection in the glass door of Agnes's Cut 'n' Curl. He saw his squeezed-up eyebrows and his turned-down mouth, and he knew there was only one word for that look. Worry.

Randall Mackey's secret was starting to stir up a little cloud of worry. And Randall knew that sometimes little clouds turn into big storms.

6

"'Cause I got a piece of paper that says so, Iris," Miss Frieda was saying to Randall's mother. "*I'm* the one here in Foley that takes in the children. Can't just anybody up and keep a baby like that."

Her voice was loud and gravelly, booming down to Randall and Jaybird from the porch above them.

The floorboards squeaked and groaned as the women rocked. Back and forth. Back and forth. One of them rocked faster than the others. Randall figured it was Miss Frieda. Her voice sounded like the voice of someone who was rocking fast.

"You're right, Frieda," Randall's mother said. "But maybe there's no harm in Charlotte tending to that child for a day or two."

"She's had that baby over a week now."

"That's right, Frieda," Jaybird's mother said. "She *has* had that baby for a week."

"*Over* a week," Miss Frieda said. "She ought to be made to do the right thing instead of whatever she dern well pleases." The rocking chair was moving faster now. "She's got no intention of doing what's right," she added.

"Preacher Ron said they reported everything like they were supposed to," Mrs. Mackey said.

"Iris," Miss Frieda said, "pardon me if I stir up some muddy water here, but that preacher man's got a way of making everything sound like a gift from heaven sent special delivery to him and that wife of his."

Randall sat still, waiting. He could picture his mama's face: pinched up and twitching. All anybody had to do to get a rise out of her was to say something bad about Preacher Ron.

"Well, Frieda," Randall's mother said, "you *are* caring for an awful lot of children right now. I can't see why you're making such a fuss about Charlotte keeping just *one*."

Back and forth the conversation went. Every so often, Mrs. Gilley said, "That's right" or "Uh-huh!" Randall and Jaybird grinned at each other every time Miss Frieda said something nasty, like when she called Mrs. Jennings a high-and-mighty starched shirt. Then when she said Mrs. Jennings thought she could stick her head in a bucket of slop and come out smelling like a rose, they had to cover their heads with a beach towel to keep from laughing out loud.

"Let's go see if T.J. and them are shootin' hoops," Jaybird whispered to Randall under the towel.

Randall shook his head. "Naw, it's too hot."

Outside, the air was thick with heat, but under the porch, it was cool and damp. The scraggly marigolds along the edge of the porch were dried up and brown. From his dug-out seat in the dirt of the fort, Randall could see the steamy heat rising up off the street in waves. The asphalt basketball court behind the school would be even hotter. Besides, Randall wanted to stay and hear what else the women were going to say about Moses.

Jaybird threw the beach towel off their heads and lay back in the dirt.

"Who you think oughtta take care of Moses?" he whispered.

"His mama, I reckon."

"Naw, I mean if his mama is gone for good."

"She's not gone for good," Randall said.

"How do you know?"

"Why would anybody just up and leave their baby like that? Think about it, Jaybird."

"Shoot, Randall, sometimes you ain't got a lick of sense," Jaybird said. "Mamas leave babies all the time. Why do you think Miss Frieda has all them kids?"

The rocking chairs stopped rocking, and the porch

steps creaked. Randall and Jaybird watched Miss Frieda's ugly brown shoes go down the steps and up the sidewalk. The screen door above them slammed when Mrs. Gilley and Mrs. Mackey went inside.

Randall and Jaybird started to crawl out from under the porch but stopped when they heard Althea's voice.

"Hey, Miss Frieda."

"Althea. How you doin', lamb?"

"I'm doing fine, but T.J. ain't."

"What you mean?"

"He lit a firecracker and made somebody cry."

"A firecracker?" Miss Frieda hollered. "Who cried?"

"Inez Dawson," Althea said. "And then her big ole son come out and grabbed T.J. You know her son? That man named Henry?"

Randall and Jaybird watched through the lattice as Miss Frieda stormed off up the street, her shorts making a swish, swish, swish noise.

Althea skipped toward the porch, clutching a paper bag.

"I got somethin' *y'all* want," she sang into the fort.

"Oh, yeah?" Jaybird hollered through the lattice. "Well, that's good, 'cause we want something to make you drop dead and disappear."

"Okay," Althea said. "I reckon I'll just give these ole firecrackers to somebody who wants 'em."

Randall and Jaybird scrambled out from under the porch.

"Give me that," Jaybird said, grabbing for the bag.

"It's mine." Althea jerked the bag behind her back.

"Give it here."

Jaybird dove for Althea's legs, knocking her into the dirt with an "Oompf."

"Get that bag, Randall," he called out while he held Althea down. Her skinny legs kicked and flailed in the air.

Randall looked up at the porch to make sure Mrs. Gilley and his mama hadn't come back out. Then he snatched the bag away from Althea and peered inside.

"It *is* firecrackers," he said.

Jaybird shook Althea's shoulders. "Where'd you get them firecrackers?"

"T.J. give 'em to me."

"How come?"

" 'Cause that man Henry was gonna bust him one for scarin' Mrs. Dawson, and T.J. was crying and all and saying it wasn't him and then he threw that bag to me and I come on home."

Althea grabbed at the bag, but Randall jerked it away from her.

"I hate you, Randall Mackey," Althea said. "And you ain't invited to the party for Moses."

45

"What party?"

"The party I'm having when I baby-sit."

"You lie like a rug, Althea," Jaybird said.

"I do not."

"I already told you, Althea. Nobody's gonna let a ninny-brain diaper head like you baby-sit."

"I am too." Althea stamped her foot. "I'm gonna be a mother's helper, and I start tomorrow."

"Tomorrow is church day," Jaybird said.

"I know that, you smelly rat-breath baby," Althea said. "I get to hold Moses while Mrs. Jennings sings with the Celebration Choir. And then when I win the Bible drill, I get to be a mother's helper every Sunday."

"What if you don't win the Bible drill?" Randall said.

"I *am* winning." Althea tossed her head and skipped off down the sidewalk.

That night, Randall crawled way down under his sheet with a flashlight. He made a fist and inspected it. Then he tried to draw it. Fists were tricky, but he kept trying until he got it right. Then he drew another fist. Perfect, he thought. Two punching fists. One black, one white. Then, up at the top, he drew the floppy hat and the wild black hair, looking down at the two angry fists.

7

And what else do you think needs to be planted in your Garden of Life?" Preacher Ron said.

He put both hands on the pulpit and leaned over to gaze out at the congregation. The room grew quiet. A few church bulletins flapped as folks fanned themselves. Someone coughed. A ceiling fan whirred lazily above them.

Preacher Ron had already told them about how they needed to plant plenty of peas, like "politeness" and "prayer." And then they needed squash in their Gardens of Life, to squash gossip and squash lies.

The room was so still and quiet Randall could hear Carl Langley's wheezy breathing from way in the back row.

"LETTUCE!" Preacher Ron hollered, making a few folks jump.

He leaned farther over the pulpit and said almost in a whisper, *"Let us* be faithful."

Randall's mother nodded.

"Let us be unselfish."

Nod. "Amen."

"And *let us* LOVE one another."

All around the room folks raised their hands and said, "Amen."

"But our Gardens of Life need one more thing," Preacher Ron said.

Randall tried to think what it could be. Corn? Naw. Potatoes? Probably not.

"TURNIPS!" Preacher Ron shouted.

Randall's daddy chuckled and poked Randall in the ribs. Some kid laughed out real loud. Randall figured it was probably Althea.

"TURN UP for church," Preacher Ron said, grinning out at everyone.

"And TURN UP with a smile."

"Amen, brother," Mrs. Mackey said.

Preacher Ron went on some more about pulling the weeds of evil habits and bad tempers out of your Garden of Life, and then he called Hank Dowlings up to give the announcements.

Hank gave the Sunday school attendance report and the score of the softball game with the Gospel Light Church over in Aiken. He announced the next

Partners in Prayer meeting and gave an update on the cost of repairs to the church bus. He reminded all the young people about the Junior Bible Drill next Sunday night, and then he asked if anyone had any questions.

Someone in the back of the room called out, "Any word on finding that baby's mama?"

Randall felt his heart pounding in his chest. He kept his eyes on the hymnal in his lap so nobody could see what surely must have been written right there plain as day on his face: "*I* know who left that baby in the cardboard box."

"Well now, Howard," Preacher Ron said. "I'm glad you asked that."

He looked over at Mrs. Jennings sitting in the front row.

"Charlotte and I have reported everything to the authorities, and now all we can do is take care of little Moses like we were chosen to do," he said.

Mrs. Jennings set a smile on her face and nodded, glancing around the room. Her blond French twist glittered with hair spray. Then she stood up and faced the congregation and asked that baby Moses be cradled in the arms of the Rock of Ages Baptist Church.

"He is a lamb in need of a flock," she said.

Randall fidgeted on the hard pew. His mother put her hand on his knee and gave him a look that meant "Quit that fidgeting."

Then Mrs. Jennings announced that the winner of the Junior Bible Drill would get to take care of Moses every week during choir practice. Randall looked back at Althea. She was sitting up straight and stiff, with yellow bows on every braid. She grinned and wiggled her white-gloved fingers at him.

After church, Randall waited in the Fellowship Hall for Jaybird.

"I told you I was gonna be a mother's helper every Sunday," Althea said.

Randall wrapped some brownies in a paper napkin. "You have to win the Bible drill first," he said.

"I *am* winning the Bible drill."

"How do you know?"

"I just know." Althea licked frosting off a cupcake.

Jaybird tiptoed up behind her and yelled, "Boo!"

Althea just kept licking that cupcake like she hadn't even heard him.

"Mama said you have to help her pack up Queenie's lunch," Jaybird said to Althea. He loosened his tie and examined the dessert table.

"You can't have the peach cobbler," Althea said. "It's only for grownups."

Jaybird scooped peach cobbler onto a paper plate.

"I'm tellin'." Althea disappeared into the crowd of folks clustered in groups around the Fellowship Hall.

"What you want to do today?" Jaybird asked Randall.

Randall shrugged. "I don't know. What do you want to do?"

Jaybird shrugged. "I don't know."

Just then the sound of Jaybird's mother's voice could be heard above the noise of the crowd.

"Says who, Charlotte?" she was saying.

Randall looked over to where a group of women huddled around a playpen.

"Come on." He motioned for Jaybird to follow him.

The two boys made their way over to where the women were. Moses kicked and gurgled on a rainbow-colored quilt in the playpen.

"It seems fairly obvious, Lottie," Mrs. Jennings said to Jaybird's mother. "This church was *chosen* to take care of Moses." She gestured toward the gurgling baby. Her shiny gold charm bracelet jangled up and down her arm.

Several of the women nodded at one another. A few mumbled, "That's right."

Mrs. Gilley looked down at Moses, then back up at Mrs. Jennings.

"All I'm saying, Charlotte," she said, "is that Miss Frieda has much more experience with this sort of thing. And she's *licensed* for foster care."

Moses started to whimper. Mrs. Jennings scooped him up and held him against her, jiggling him and smiling at Mrs. Gilley.

"I appreciate your concern, Lottie, really I do. But whoever the troubled soul is who gave us this child knew what she was doing."

"How do you know it was a woman that left him?" Mrs. Gilley said. "Maybe a man left that baby."

Mrs. Jennings kept jiggling Moses. "Well, one thing I *do* know is that this child wasn't left on Miss Frieda's front steps," she said.

The other women nodded at one another.

"Besides," Mrs. Jennings went on, "maybe whoever left him figured Miss Frieda had about all the children she could handle."

Mrs. Gilley kept her calm gaze on Mrs. Jennings.

"Maybe," she said. "I guess we'll know for sure when the police find whoever it was that left him."

With that, Mrs. Gilley turned and walked out of the Fellowship Hall.

The women stared after her. One of them said, "Well!"

"Let's go." Jaybird pulled Randall's elbow, but Randall stayed rooted to the floor. He watched Mrs. Jennings's face getting red and splotchy.

"Are the police really trying to find his mama?" Randall asked.

The women all turned in surprise, as if they'd never seen Randall Mackey before.

"Well, yes, Randall," Mrs. Jennings said. "I imagine they are."

"Do you think anybody knows who she is?" Randall kept his hands in his pockets and tried to look like he wasn't all that interested in the answer to that question.

Mrs. Jennings rocked Moses back and forth, smiling down at him. She ran her hand over his hair. "Well, Randall, think about it. If somebody knew who this child's mama is, they would tell us, now, wouldn't they?"

Randall struggled to keep looking like somebody who didn't know who left the baby in the cardboard box. He nodded. "Yes, ma'am, I suppose so," he said.

"Come on." Jaybird yanked Randall's arm again. "I got to go."

Randall followed Jaybird out of the Fellowship Hall. As they headed down the sidewalk toward Woodmont Street, Jaybird chattered away about a cat he'd been feeding and maybe his daddy would let him keep it and they could make a bed for it down in the fort.

But Randall wasn't listening. He was thinking. His mama was all the time saying, "Oh, what a tangled web we weave, when first we practice to deceive." But he hadn't exactly deceived anybody, had he? Naw. Not a single person.

Then how come his web was feeling so tangled?

8

That preacher man is gonna get in trouble," T.J. said.

Randall wiggled a stick around in the dirt, leaving squiggly lines in Miss Frieda's dusty yard. "How come?" he said.

"For keeping that baby."

Randall stopped wiggling the stick and looked at T.J.

"What do you mean?"

"Them church people can't keep Moses. They ain't licensed to have foster kids."

"How do you know?" Jaybird asked. He fiddled with the dial of a beat-up radio on the porch. Every now and then a crackly, static noise spewed out of it.

"Miss Frieda said so," T.J. said.

Randall tossed the stick into the street. "Maybe they got a license and Miss Frieda doesn't know about it."

T.J. shook his head. "Naw," he said. "She knows. She went over to Spartanburg to the foster care office." T.J. threw a rock up onto the roof of the house. It rolled down and dropped onto the porch beside Jaybird.

"Why'd she do that?" Jaybird asked.

T.J. shrugged. "I don't know. But she said just 'cause Preacher Ron and Mrs. Jennings are church folks don't mean they can break the law." He threw another rock. This one went clear over the top of the house and landed with a clatter on the garbage cans in the alley. "She said anybody else in Foley would've been made to give that baby up to her and Earlene." He scratched in the dirt for another rock. "Besides," he added, "she says he belongs with his own kind."

"How come?" Randall said.

T.J. shrugged. "Just does, that's all."

They all looked up at the sound of feet slapping against the sidewalk. Althea was running toward them. She was wearing a bathing suit and shiny black church shoes with ruffly pink socks. Instead of her usual braids, her hair stood out in a fluffy black halo around her head.

"Guess what?" she said.

Randall, Jaybird, and T.J. waited.

"There's a policeman over at the church," Althea said, taking big gulps of air to catch her breath.

Randall's heart began to thump hard inside his chest. "What for?" he said.

Althea swatted gnats away from her face. "I bet Mrs. Jennings is going to prison."

"Prison!" Randall's heart had gone from a trot to a gallop.

Althea nodded, her eyes wide with excitement. "I bet she is."

Jaybird got up off the porch and came down into the yard. "Althea, get your dogmeat face on out of here." He tossed a rock at Althea, hitting her in the knee.

She grabbed her knee and hopped around the yard, yelling, "OWWWWW!" Then she picked up a bigger rock and hurled it at Jaybird. It whizzed past him and onto the porch, hitting T.J.'s radio.

"Now look what you done," Jaybird hollered.

"You're paying for that," T.J. said, jabbing a finger at Althea.

"Y'all hush up," Randall said. He turned to Althea. "What's the policeman doing?"

"Taking Mrs. Jennings to prison," Althea said with a grin.

Jaybird kicked dirt at Althea. "You better go weed your garden, booger brain, 'cause you got some big ole LIES growing in there."

"I don't care what you think, Jaybird Gilley." Althea

turned to Randall. "Your mama said you got to go over to Mr. Avery's and pick up some dirty sheets and stuff." She held her nose in a pee-yew kind of way. Then she tossed her head and skipped off down the sidewalk. Even after she had disappeared around the corner, they could still hear her singing.

"This little light of mine,
I'm gonna let it shine . . ."

Randall knocked on Mr. Avery's door. He could hear the television playing loudly inside. Probably Queenie watching soap operas. Sometimes she talked to the ladies all dressed up in their furs and diamonds and stuff.

"He's lying to you, you bimbo," she'd say. "Can't you tell a cheater when you see one?"

When Mr. Avery opened the door, Randall was surprised at how old and tired he looked.

"Hey, Mr. Avery," Randall said. "I came to get the laundry."

"Aw, now, I don't want your mama doing my laundry," he said.

"She wants to."

"Well, I admit it sure is a help." Mr. Avery motioned for Randall to come in. Queenie didn't look up from the television. She leaned way out of her chair, pushing her face up close to the screen. Randall could see her pink scalp through her thin gray hair.

"Ha!" she yelled at the handsome soap opera man in the black tuxedo. "Serves you right!"

Mr. Avery sank into his beat-up easy chair with a sigh. He ran his hands through his greasy hair. "It's been a long day, Randall."

"I brought this," Randall said, handing Mr. Avery his sketchbook.

Mr. Avery's face brightened. He took the book from Randall and began turning the pages.

"Well, look at this," he said. "A hermit thrush."

"Actually, that's a wood thrush," Randall said. "You can tell 'cause it has more red on its head and the spots are rounder."

"That's real nice, Randall," Mr. Avery said. "Shoot, I think you know more about birds than me now."

Randall shook his head. "Naw," he said, "I just get all that from my bird book."

Mr. Avery turned another page. "This is the finest bird nest I ever saw. Look at this, Queenie."

Queenie glanced at the sketchbook, then flapped her hand and said, "Be quiet, mister."

"It's an oriole's nest," Randall said.

"Now, what's this?" Mr. Avery asked, turning to another page.

Randall leaned forward to look at the page. His stomach balled up into a knot when he saw the drawing of the floppy straw hat.

"Oh, that's just an ole junky picture I drew one time," Randall said. "I thought I tore that out of there."

"Look at this, Queenie." Mr. Avery pushed the sketchbook in front of Queenie. She flapped her hand again, but her eyes darted to the drawing.

Her mouth opened into an "O." She narrowed her eyes and leaned down so close to the drawing that her nose nearly touched the paper. She pushed her hair out of her eyes and jabbed a finger at the drawing.

"Not her again!" she said. "What's she doing here?"

Mr. Avery chuckled. "What you talkin' about, Queenie?"

Queenie traced the drawing with her finger and nodded. "I know her," she said.

Randall's stomach flopped. He reached for the sketchbook, but Queenie clutched it against her.

"I want this," she said.

"I'll draw a better one," Randall said. "That one's no good."

"I like this hat." Queenie smiled at Randall. "I remember this hat."

Randall tugged at the sketchbook, but Queenie slapped his hand and said, "Stop it, Monroe!"

Mr. Avery put his hand on Queenie's knee. "That ain't nice, Queenie," he said. "You give Randall his book."

Queenie tossed the book at Randall and stomped into the bedroom. Mr. Avery turned his sad eyes toward Randall. "Sorry about that, son," he said.

"That's okay."

"It's a nice hat," Mr. Avery said.

Randall tore the page out of the sketchbook. He folded it and tucked it into his pocket.

"Mr. Avery," Randall said, "what would you do if some bad stuff started happening and you could make it stop if you told a secret? Only, if you told the secret, then something *else* bad might happen?"

Now, why had he gone and said that, Randall wondered. He sure never meant to. He watched Mr. Avery's bushy gray eyebrows arch up and a look of pure puzzlement come on his face.

Randall looked down at the faded green carpet. On the television, some woman was singing about how clean her clothes were.

Mr. Avery scratched his whiskery chin. Finally he said, "Hmmm, that's a hard one." He scratched his chin some more. "A bad thing happening if you don't tell, and a bad thing happening if you do. Right?"

"Right."

"Hmmmmmm." Mr. Avery kept scratching his

chin. "First off, I'd remind myself to be careful about tellin' stuff."

"What do you mean?"

"Well, son, lettin' the cat out of the bag is a whole lot easier than puttin' it back in." Mr. Avery leaned toward Randall. "You know what I mean?"

"I think so."

"Next," Mr. Avery went on, "I'd ask myself a question."

"What question?"

"I'd ask myself which would be worse, telling the secret or not telling the secret. And then . . ."

Mr. Avery sat back in his easy chair and folded his hands in his lap.

"Yeah?" Randall said. "And then what?"

"And then I'd do the right thing."

Randall felt a big lump of disappointment plop down inside him.

"But how would you know what the right thing was?"

Mr. Avery looked at Randall with his sad, watery eyes. "I'm afraid I ain't got an answer for that," he said.

▰ ▰ ▰

Randall took the long way home. The heavy basket of laundry bumped against his knees as he walked. By the time he got home, he had a picture in his head. He went straight back to his bedroom and pulled the drawing of the straw hat out of his pocket. He smoothed it out on his desk and opened his tattered box of colored pencils. He turned the paper over and drew a lady with a blond French twist.

He sat back to examine it. "Yep," he thought, "that looks just like Mrs. Charlotte Jennings." He used his ruler to draw a thick black square around her. He made up-and-down lines from the top of the box to the bottom, right over Mrs. Jennings. Like prison bars.

He sat back and looked at Mrs. Jennings in prison. Then he laid his head down on his desk and thought and thought about doing the right thing. But no matter how hard he tried, he just couldn't figure out what the right thing was.

9

Before long, it seemed like Foley, South Carolina, was split right down the middle. One side made no bones about the fact that they thought Moses should most definitely be with Miss Frieda. The other side was of the strong opinion that Mrs. Charlotte Jennings was the one who should be taking care of Moses.

And right in the middle of all that arguing was Randall Mackey, whose insides were flip-flopping around like a trout on a riverbank.

Finally one day he just up and asked Miss Frieda, "What if somebody knows who left Moses at the church but isn't telling?"

He used all his willpower to keep his face looking calm and innocent, but he didn't have enough willpower to stop himself from blushing. He could feel the red creeping up his neck, across his cheeks, and right on up to the top of his head.

Miss Frieda didn't seem to notice. She let out a snort.

"I'd say that person sure in tarnation better have some grits and gumption," she said.

"How come?"

" 'Cause if somebody knows who that baby's mama is but is just sitting back and watching us get all riled up like this . . ." Miss Frieda paused.

Randall leaned toward her, waiting.

". . . then it would take grits and gumption to do the right thing and fess up," she said.

There it was again. *The right thing.* Randall studied the dirty steps of Miss Frieda's porch.

"What if that person doesn't have any grits and gumption?" he said.

Miss Frieda fanned herself with a *Reader's Digest.* "Then that person would be some kinda low-lying liver-bellied buzzard bait." She squinted her eyes at Randall and added, "Don't you think?"

Randall shrugged. "I reckon."

Miss Frieda slapped her knee and laughed so loud her mangy old hound dog scurried out from under the shrubbery and stared at them. She put her arm around Randall and squeezed him against her. She smelled like bacon grease and talcum powder all mixed together.

"I swannee, Randall Mackey," she said, "you're about the most serious child I've ever seen in all my born days."

Randall put a smile on his face and made himself let out a little chuckle.

Miss Frieda jiggled his shoulder. "Seems to me like we need to get our lives back to the way they supposed to be instead of all fired up at each other every dang minute of the day. Maybe I ought not to be making such a fuss. I know Charlotte wants a child of her own. But that child's not hers, and—"

T.J. burst through the screen door and grinned at Miss Frieda. "Cora Lee spilled a whole bag of flour on the kitchen floor," he said.

"You think that's funny, Tyrone Jamal?" she said, grunting as she pushed herself up off the steps.

T.J. wiped the grin off his face real quick. "No, ma'am," he said. "Can I go now? I finished them chores."

Miss Frieda flapped her hand at him and said, "Go on," before disappearing through the screen door.

"What you wanna do?" T.J. said to Randall.

"Let's go over to Jaybird's."

They raced up the alley to the Gilleys' house. Jaybird sat on the edge of the porch, dangling his legs over the side. Althea stood on top of two rusty tin cans with a

65

long loop of string tied to each one. She held the strings and took high, jerky steps up and down the sidewalk. The cans came down with a clank.

"What y'all doing?" Randall asked.

"I got stilts," Althea said. She held up a foot and showed Randall the can. "And Jaybird has to help me win the Bible drill."

Jaybird waved a piece of paper at Randall and T.J. "I'm asking Bible questions and then she's gonna get me some more firecrackers."

"I *might* get firecrackers," Althea said. She took a few stiff, jerky steps on her tin-can stilts. Clank, clank, clank.

"Ask me another one," she said to Jaybird.

Jaybird studied the paper in his hand. "Okay, say that Proverbs verse you kept missing last night."

"Aw, that's easy." Althea jumped up and down on the tin-can stilts while she shouted, " 'He that spareth his rod hateth his son: but he that loveth him chasteneth him betimes.' "

"Betimes?" T.J. said. "What's that?"

"Hush up, Tyrone Jamal," Althea said.

"Well, what *is* 'betimes,' Miss Bible Queen Genius?" Jaybird said. "You're supposed to know what all the words mean."

"Be-TIMES," Althea said, "means like there *be-*

times when you want to chasteneth and there *betimes* when you don't want to chasteneth." She glared at T.J. "Any idiot knows that."

T.J. grinned and poked Randall.

"Then what does 'chasteneth' mean?" Randall said.

Althea galloped away from them on her tin-can stilts. When she got to the end of the sidewalk, she turned and said over her shoulder, "If you don't know, I ain't tellin' you, Randall Mackey."

Just then Miss Frieda came storming up the walk toward them. Her fists were balled up at the end of her big, stiff arms, and her shorts went swish, swish, swish as she came closer.

T.J.'s eyes widened. "Uh-oh," he said. "What'd I do now?"

But Miss Frieda swished right past T.J. and Randall. She nearly knocked Althea plumb off her stilts. She stomped up the steps without even looking at Jaybird and banged on the Gilleys' screen door.

Mrs. Gilley came to the door wiping her hands on a dish towel. Before she could say anything, Miss Frieda said, "That gol-dern church has got *some* kinda nerve."

"What you talking about?" Mrs. Gilley held the screen door open and motioned Miss Frieda inside.

Randall raced over to the side of the house and crouched under the open window to listen. Jaybird and

T.J. joined him, crawling behind the shrubbery on their hands and knees. Randall motioned for them to keep quiet, but Althea was making so much noise with her clanging tin cans that Randall could catch only bits and pieces of what Miss Frieda was telling Mrs. Gilley.

". . . them social workers from Spartanburg came down and . . ."

". . . must think she don't have to be licensed like everybody else . . ."

". . . ought to take that child away from her . . ."

Every now and then Mrs. Gilley would say, "Well, I never," or "Don't that just take the cake?"

"I'm telling you, Lottie," Miss Frieda said, "that woman thinks she don't have to do things like the rest of us just 'cause she's a preacher's wife. She's got them folks up in Spartanburg letting her rule the roost and making everybody think she's got the keys to the Pearly Gates."

Mrs. Gilley muttered some indignant words of sympathy, and then Miss Frieda's hollering came right out the window clear as anything.

"Maybe them folks up there need to learn that the bucket always brings up what's in the well," she said.

Randall looked at Jaybird and T.J. What did that mean, he wondered. Jaybird cupped his hand over his mouth to stifle a giggle.

The boys had been so busy trying to hear Miss Frieda that they hadn't noticed that Althea had disappeared. Suddenly those tin cans clomped down the porch steps.

"Miss Frieda said she's going right to the top," Althea called out.

"What's that mean?" Randall asked, brushing dirt off his knees.

"It means she's calling the FBI to take Mrs. Jennings to prison for kidnapping Moses." Althea hopped off her tin cans and began swinging them over her head by the strings. Randall had to duck as the cans whipped around.

Jaybird and T.J. crawled out from behind the shrubbery.

"Yeah, right, Althea," Jaybird said. "Like anybody believes *you*."

"And when the FBI finds Moses' mama, *she's* going to prison, too," Althea said. " 'Cause it's against the law to leave your baby in a box."

"How're they gonna find his mama?" Randall asked.

"Miss Frieda's gonna keep lookin', but she's got to hurry up 'cause she's gonna die." The tin cans made a whirring sound as Althea swung them around and around over her head.

Jaybird jumped up and grabbed for the strings, pulling the cans down with a clang. "What you talking about?" he said.

Althea yanked the tin cans away from Jaybird and began to swing them back and forth, closer and closer to Jaybird with each swing.

"Miss Frieda's gonna find that baby's mama if it kills her, and the way she's been feeling lately, it's liable to. And then Mrs. Jennings will get to keep that baby over Miss Frieda's dead body."

Althea swung the cans harder. "*And*," she said, pushing her chin up and glaring over at Randall, "she said Moses belongs with his own kind instead of over there with them highfalutin do-gooders at that church." She stopped swinging the cans and pranced off toward the house. When she got to the porch steps, she stopped and said, "I heard her with my very own two ears." Then she disappeared into the house, dragging the clanging cans along behind her.

Jaybird and T.J. were laughing and carrying on, but Randall didn't think what Althea said was so funny. Randall was feeling his worry get bigger and bigger. Everything was turning into a big, scary mess—and all he had to do was say, "I know who left the baby in the cardboard box on the front steps of the Rock of Ages Baptist Church."

But he couldn't.

10

I know y'all will want to join me in congratulating Miss Maddie Shadd on her fine, fine performance in the Junior Bible Drill last night." Preacher Ron smiled down at the beaming girl. She pushed her shiny red hair behind her ears and waved a gloved hand at the congregation. Everyone clapped. Someone called out, "Thatta girl, Maddie!"

Randall looked back at the Gilleys. Althea was slumped so far down in the pew that only the top of her head was showing.

Preacher Ron nodded at Maddie. "Why don't you recite those verses about the sluggard?" he said, then turned to the congregation and added, "That was the final question that made Miss Maddie here our Junior Bible Drill champion."

Maddie jabbed the toe of her shiny white shoe into

the floor and did a little curtsy, holding her long, yellow skirt out like butterfly wings. Then she stood up straight and stiff, lifted her chin in the air, and called out, " 'Go to the ant, thou sluggard; consider her ways, and be wise.' "

She paused while folks clapped. Then she cleared her throat and added, "Proverbs 6, verse 6."

From the back of the church came loud, thunking noises. Everyone turned to look at Mrs. Gilley glaring down at Althea.

Maddie smoothed her hair again and recited, " 'As vinegar to the tooth, and as smoke to the eyes—' "

Althea jumped up and pumped her fist in the air. " *'Teeth'!*" she hollered. " 'As vinegar to the *teeth.*' "

She grinned at the congregation, then added, "Ha!" before sitting down again.

Randall felt a twinge of excitement. Church was usually so boring it was fun having something out of the ordinary happen. All around him, folks were whispering and shaking their heads and wagging their fingers at Althea. Randall's father chuckled, and Mrs. Mackey poked him.

After Preacher Ron gave Maddie her shiny gold Junior Bible Drill medal, he told her she was now the official helper for Baby Moses.

Mrs. Jennings smiled and bounced Moses on her lap.

Then Preacher Ron motioned for Maddie to sit down and he began to preach.

"I call today's sermon 'CHILDREN Are Our TREASURED Gifts.' "

He was using his preaching way of talking, hollering out the important words and saying the others real low and soft so everybody had to lean forward a little to hear.

"I know because the BIBLE tells us so in the Book of Psalms, chapter 127, verse 3," he said.

"In fact," Preacher Ron continued, "did y'all know that the word 'CHILDREN' appears in the Bible FOUR HUNDRED AND EIGHTY-TWO TIMES?"

He pounded his fist on the pulpit with each word, then paused.

Randall wondered if Preacher Ron had actually counted all those words in the Bible.

"THAT is how important children are to this church," he went on.

A couple of folks hollered out, "Amen."

"Their souls are precious to us," Preacher Ron said softly. "They are the FUTURE of this church."

"Yes, brother," someone called from the back of the church.

"And so I say to you that we must stand firm and accept our role as FAMILY to a child who was given to us by a troubled soul."

Uh-oh. Randall felt that worry knot tumbling around inside him. He squeezed his eyes shut and recited to himself, "Don't talk about Moses. Don't talk about Moses."

But Preacher Ron did talk about Moses. On and on and on. And then suddenly he was talking about troublemakers.

"We must AVOID the troublemakers," he said. "The Second Book of Thessalonians tells us so."

Mrs. Jennings nodded and called out, "That's right."

Then Preacher Ron started pounding the pulpit loud and hard and saying how troublemakers were trying to take Moses away from this church family.

And that's when Mrs. Gilley yanked Jaybird and Althea up by their collars, and marched right up the aisle and out the door.

Later that day, Randall and Jaybird lay on the blue tarp under the Gilleys' porch. Randall rested his head on his hands and stared up at the damp, mildewed boards above them.

"Do you think your mama really means it?" he asked Jaybird.

"Uh-huh." Jaybird tossed a wadded-up candy wrapper from hand to hand. "She says she ain't never stepping so much as a big toe in that church again. She says Preacher Ron is trying to poison our minds with lies about Miss Frieda."

"This sure is a mess."

"Yeah," Jaybird said, "all 'cause of one stupid baby."

"Yeah."

"I wish that baby's mama would come and take him home," Jaybird said.

"Yeah." Randall nodded. "I wish she would, too."

▬ ▬ ▬

That night, Randall crawled up under the covers with his sketchbook and flashlight. He drew a bird, but it looked funny, so he scribbled over it. He started drawing a house, but it was boring, so he erased it. Then he began to draw himself. He was good at drawing himself because he had practiced a lot, staring in the mirror as he outlined his mousy brown hair hanging down over his ears and his nose that was too big for his face. When he got to his mouth, he drew it open, like he was talking. Like maybe he was telling his secret. Then he drew a big circle coming out of his mouth, and in the circle he wrote: LAVONIA SHIRLEY.

It felt so good to write those words that he traced over the letters two more times. Then he took a black marker and scribbled over them. Back and forth, back and forth, until all that was left was a big black blob.

He turned off the flashlight and lay back on his pillow. He closed his eyes and whispered his prayers. After asking for all his usual stuff, Randall asked for grits and gumption.

But when he opened his eyes, he still felt like some kind of low-lying, liver-bellied buzzard bait.

11

Randall wanted everything to go back to the way it used to be. He wanted everybody to stop taking sides and arguing and acting downright hateful. He wanted the Gilleys to sit in the sixth row on the left side at church. And he wanted his mom to sit on Mrs. Gilley's front porch and drink iced tea and talk about kids and husbands and the best place to buy ground beef.

But no matter how hard Randall wished for it, he couldn't make it happen. Everybody kept arguing, the Gilleys stopped coming to church, and his mom didn't visit Mrs. Gilley anymore.

"I don't have to sit there and listen to her and Miss Frieda talk ugly about my church," Mrs. Mackey told Randall.

Sometimes she would come over to the Gilleys' to tell Randall to go home for supper. She would nod at Mrs. Gilley and say, "Evening, Lottie."

"Evening, Iris," Mrs. Gilley would say from her rocking chair on the porch.

"Time for supper, Randall," Mrs. Mackey would say, then turn and head back up the sidewalk.

Randall would look at Jaybird, and Jaybird would shrug. And Randall would feel awful. He missed the friendly chatter between their mothers. But more than that, he missed the Gilleys in church.

"I'm glad we ain't going there no more," Althea said. "I hate that church."

"You better stop saying that, Althea," Jaybird said. "It's bad luck to say that."

"I don't care."

"Lightning's gonna come down and zap you right on the head."

"So?" Althea said. "I do hate that church." She poked her tongue out of the corner of her mouth while she colored her fingernails with a purple marker.

"How come?" Randall said.

" 'Cause everybody at that church is stupid," Althea said. "Especially Maddie Shadd."

"You're just mad 'cause you lost that Bible drill," Jaybird said.

"I am not."

"You are too." Jaybird poked Randall. "I guess she ain't as smart as she thought she was, huh, Randall?"

Althea lunged at Jaybird and swiped her marker

across the front of his T-shirt, leaving a squiggly purple line. Jaybird yanked the marker away from her and tossed it up on the roof of the house.

"Everybody knows what the longest chapter in the Bible is," Jaybird said.

Althea chose another marker and began coloring her fingernails again. Orange.

"Psalm 119," she said.

"Too late, dumbo," Jaybird said. "You should have said that in the Bible drill."

"So, who cares?" Althea said. "Not me."

Randall drew in the dirt with a stick. A cat. A bicycle. A wheelbarrow.

"Church is boring without you," Randall said to Jaybird.

"Yeah," Jaybird said. "And we gotta ride all the way over to Duncan Springs with a bunch of people I don't even know to go to a church that ain't even got an organ."

"Yeah," Althea said. Then she jumped in the middle of Randall's dirt drawings and shuffled her feet around, sending dust swirling in the air around them.

━━ ━━ ━━

That Sunday, Randall sat in church and drew a flock of geese flying in a V shape across the page of his notebook. Preacher Ron preached and the Celebration Choir sang and folks hollered out "Amen" and "Praise be." Randall just kept on drawing, even when Smokey

Dobbins got dunked in the baptismal pool and came up sputtering and coughing and carrying on.

Every now and then, he looked back at the sixth row on the left, but the Gilleys weren't there. He watched a fly settle on the shoulder of the lady in front of him. He counted how many times Arthur Bennings blew his nose. He tapped his pencil in time to the hymns. Then he glanced out the window, and his heart dropped clear down to his stomach.

He sat up straight and craned his neck to see better. Maybe he was just imagining things.

Nope. He wasn't. A woman sat on the curb across the street from the church. A woman wearing a floppy straw hat.

Randall jerked his head around to see if anybody else was looking at the woman in the hat. No one was. Everyone else was singing or yawning or whispering to their squirming kids.

Randall felt his heart bumping inside him. He looked out the window again.

The woman stood up and stared over at the church. For a minute, Randall thought she was looking right at him. He looked away. He joined in the singing. "Yes, we'll gather at the river, the beautiful, the beautiful river . . ."

When he looked out the window again, the lady in the straw hat was gone.

12

Randall and Jaybird each held a handle of the laundry basket as they headed toward Thomas and Sons Insurance Agency. Althea trotted along behind them.

"Let's see if we can take Queenie somewhere," she said.

"Like where?" Randall said.

"To the Winn-Dixie to buy Hershey bars with almonds. That's what she likes."

"Okay."

It was past suppertime, and the insurance agency was closed. Randall, Jaybird, and Althea headed around back to the alley. The back door was propped open with a milk crate. Just as they got there, Mr. Avery came out carrying a wastebasket.

"Well, hey there," he said. "What y'all doing?"

"We brought your laundry," Randall said.

Mr. Avery shuffled over to a nearby Dumpster and

emptied the wastebasket. His baggy pants hung down so low they dragged on the ground as he walked.

"I appreciate that. You thank your mama for me, Randall," he said. "Let's go in. I bet Queenie would like to see y'all."

When they stepped inside the back door of the office, they could hear Queenie singing down in the Averys' basement apartment.

"She'll be comin' round the mountain when she comes . . ." Loud. The same verse over and over again.

When they came into the apartment, she stopped.

"I've been looking for that," she said, pointing to the laundry basket.

"Look who's here to see you, Queenie," Mr. Avery said. "Your favorite friends."

"They took that from me." She jabbed a finger at the laundry basket. "My mother gave me that."

"That's our laundry," Mr. Avery said. "Ain't that nice?"

"Well, I don't know why they keep taking it when I told them to stop."

Althea slapped her hands over her mouth and hunched her shoulders up, trying to stifle a giggle.

Queenie picked at the tiny balls of lint on the sleeve of her sweater. Randall wondered how she could stand wearing a sweater in the summer, but she didn't seem to mind.

"We'll take Queenie to get Hershey bars," Althea said.

Queenie stopped picking at the lint and looked up. "I'll go," she said, and hurried into the bedroom.

She came out with her purse.

"You have to wear shoes," Althea said, pointing at Queenie's feet.

Queenie leaned over and looked down at her sagging black socks. Then she straightened up and frowned at Althea.

"Who told you that?" she said.

Althea looked at Mr. Avery.

"Hang on, now, Queenie," he said. "Don't run out of here yet."

He disappeared into the bedroom and came back with a pair of beat-up moccasins. He put them on the floor in front of Queenie. She slipped her feet into them and said, "Thank you, mister."

Mr. Avery tucked two dollars in her hand and kissed her on the forehead.

"Bring me a candy bar, okay?" he said.

Queenie pushed him away and hurried out the door.

On the way home from the Winn-Dixie, Althea and Queenie sang. Every now and then Queenie would stop and take a bite of her candy bar.

"She sure likes chocolate, huh?" Jaybird said.

"Yeah," Randall said. He watched her eat the candy, and thought about how she used to bake. Cupcakes and cookies and pies. And always with chocolate in them. One time she made a giant chocolate chip cookie for all the children in Vacation Bible School. But then she started making mistakes. Like leaving out the flour or putting in a dozen eggs instead of two. When she left cupcakes in the oven so long they caught on fire, Mr. Avery had to make her stop baking. She got so mad she didn't say one word for four whole days. But then Mr. Avery brought home Hershey bars with almonds and Queenie stopped being mad.

"Come on, Queenie," Randall said. "We got to get home before dark."

"Where's Lavonia?" Queenie said.

Randall felt his face grow hot. "Come on, Queenie."

"Where's Lavonia?" Queenie repeated.

"Who's Lavonia?" Jaybird said.

Randall shrugged. "Who knows? Probably somebody from a long time ago."

"You know Lavonia," Queenie said to Randall. "That one with the hat."

Randall tried to make his face look relaxed, but he could feel a little twitch by his right eye.

"Oh, *that* Lavonia," he said. "She's gone."

"Who's Lavonia?" Althea said.

"This lady that used to live around here," Randall said. "But she moved away."

"I saw her," Queenie said.

"Naw," Randall said. "You didn't see her. She's gone."

"I saw her and that box," Queenie said.

"What box?" Althea said. She crumpled up a candy wrapper and licked each finger with loud smacking noises.

They all stood there, watching Queenie. Randall tried to think of something to say to make Queenie stop talking about Lavonia.

But before he could think of anything, Queenie shuffled off down the sidewalk, clutching her purse with both hands.

On the way home from Thomas and Sons Insurance Agency, Randall tried to keep talking. About the stifling hot weather. About the kittens that had been born under T.J.'s porch. About the colored pencils he was saving his money for. About anything he could think of to keep Jaybird and Althea from asking about Lavonia.

But it didn't work.

"Who's that Lavonia lady Queenie was talking about?" Jaybird said.

Randall shrugged. "Aw, just some lady that used to live near here."

"Where'd she go?"

"I think she moved in with some of her kin out there off Highway 14," Randall said.

"I wonder why Queenie was talking about her."

"Aw, you know Queenie," Randall said. "She talks crazy."

"Yeah," Jaybird said.

Randall was glad when Jaybird stopped talking about Lavonia. He need to concentrate on the thought that kept popping into his head. He had been trying to push it away, but now he let it settle down and sit there for a spell. The thought was this: I've got to do something about Moses.

After a while it seemed like just *thinking* about doing something about Moses let in a little tiny spark of feeling better. But the problem was, *what* could he do about Moses? And if he thought of something to do, then *when* should he do it? And if he thought of when to do it, then *how* should he do it?

It seemed like every time one question popped up, along came another one. By the time Randall got home, all those questions were buzzing around inside his head like flies in a barnyard. And no matter how many times he tried to shoo them away, they just kept coming back.

But the very next day something happened that made Randall stop thinking and start doing.

13

I'm starting to worry, Randall," Mr. Avery said.

But the look in his eyes said more than "worry." The look said "scared." The look made Randall feel scared, too.

"I don't know where she could be," Mr. Avery said. "She's never gone very far. I've always been able to find her." He clutched his gnarled fingers together. "But this time I'm worried she may have gone off too far."

"I bet she went to see those kittens again," Randall said.

Mr. Avery shook his head. "I looked there."

"Oh."

"She didn't even take her purse." Mr. Avery clutched Queenie's big red purse in his lap. Queenie's favorite soap opera blared from the TV.

"What about the church?" Randall said. "I bet she went there."

"Been there." Mr. Avery shook his head again. "I'm just going to have to call the police. There's no telling where she is. She was talking all crazy this morning."

Inside, Randall was thinking about how Queenie talked crazy most all the time, but he didn't say it.

"What was she talking about?" he said.

Mr. Avery stroked Queenie's purse. "Aw, you know, going on and on about Lavonia Shirley."

Randall felt his heart beat a little faster. "Lavonia Shirley?"

"Yeah, you remember that woman that used to live over there on Pritchard Street?"

"Wonder why she'd be talking about her."

"Who knows," Mr. Avery lifted his sad eyes up to look at Randall. "I guess I'll never figure out what's going on in that head of hers."

Randall's mind was whirling.

"Then maybe she went over to Pritchard Street," he said.

Mr. Avery's head shot up. "That's it!" He tossed Queenie's purse onto the couch and stood up. "Why didn't I think of that?" he said. "I bet you anything you're right."

Mr. Avery took his beat-up baseball cap off the coffee table and placed it over his scraggly hair. "I got to go," he said.

"Can I go, too?"

Mr. Avery opened the front door and said, "Sure," as he started up the basement steps.

"Mr. Avery," Randall called after him.

Mr. Avery stopped and turned back to look at Randall.

"I wouldn't ever tell anybody about Queenie wandering off, okay?" Randall said.

Mr. Avery nodded. "You're a good boy, Randall," he said.

▃▃ ▃▃ ▃▃

When Queenie saw them, she grinned and waved.

"Hey, mister," she called out.

Randall had never seen Mr. Avery move so fast. By the time they caught up to Queenie, he was breathing loud and wheezy. One hand clutched his heart, and Randall thought for sure something terrible was about to happen.

Mr. Avery hugged Queenie, and she said, "I have to get my hair done. I'm late."

"For crying out loud, Queenie," Mr. Avery said. "You trying to scare me into the grave?"

Queenie's grin dropped. "Where's my purse?"

"At home," Mr. Avery said. "Let's go get it."

"Lavonia better go get that box," Queenie said. "Don't you think so, Monroe?" She cocked her head at Randall.

Randall shrugged. "I don't know, Queenie."

"Lavonia don't live out here no more," Mr. Avery said. He took Queenie's hand and coaxed her to start walking. "She took all them young-uns of hers and moved way out on Forest Avenue. Shoot, she may not even live in Foley anymore."

Queenie nodded so hard her wispy hair bounced on top of her head. "She does."

Mr. Avery looked at Randall and rolled his eyes. "Okay, Queenie," he said. "Let's go home and get your purse."

"My purse!" Queenie hollered. Then she took off so fast Mr. Avery and Randall had to scurry to keep up with her.

<hr>

That night after supper, Randall got out his sketchbook. He turned to a blank page and began to draw. First he drew a box. Next he drew a church steeple, a fist, a straw hat, and a purse.

Then he used a black marker to draw a line from one object to the next, until they were all connected. He sat back and looked at the drawing. It looked just like a web. A giant spiderweb with all that stuff tangled up inside it. But something was missing. Something that Randall knew was important to the web.

He picked up his pencil and drew himself—right in the middle of the spiderweb.

Then he tore the page out, folded it up, and pushed it way down under his socks with the other drawings.

He turned out the lights and said his prayers. For the umpteenth time, he asked for grits and gumption.

"I need it for sure by tomorrow," he whispered into the darkness of his bedroom. " 'Cause tomorrow I'm doing something to fix this mess."

14

In the far corner of the Mackeys' garage, Randall's father had an office. At least, he called it an office. Actually, the only thing there was a teetering card table piled with moldy cardboard boxes bulging with papers. Under the card table was a metal file cabinet.

When Randall was little, he used to look through the file cabinet. It was crammed with letters, old calendars, Christmas cards, and boring magazines with titles like *Insurance Today*.

Randall was pretty sure he remembered something else that used to be in the file cabinet. A map of Foley.

He looked behind him to make sure his mother was still inside. Then he stepped over paint cans and garden tools and made his way to his father's office. He pushed a cracked flowerpot out of the way and opened the file cabinet.

He searched through the jumble of papers in the

drawer. Sure enough, he found it. "Your complimentary map of Foley, South Carolina, from your friends at Nelson's Brake and Tire Company."

Randall opened the map and smoothed it out on the garage floor. He figured he could probably find his way around the heart of Foley blindfolded. But he wasn't too sure about some of the narrow country roads that forked off the main streets and headed on out to the red-dirt fields outside of town.

Randall squinted down at the map, running his finger along the roads. Suddenly he jabbed a finger at the map. There it was. Forest Avenue. Where Lavonia Shirley had moved with all those young-uns.

Randall used his finger to trace the route from Forest Avenue, down, over, down some more, until he ended up at the spot on Woodmont Street where his own house was. How far was that, he wondered. It didn't look too far on the map, but Randall had a feeling it was farther than he had ever been by himself before. Could he ride his bike there? Maybe. But wouldn't he have to tell his mother? And wouldn't she want to know why in the world he wanted to go clear out to Forest Avenue? Of course she would.

What if he didn't tell his mother? What if he just went? Randall had never done anything like that before. Just the thought of it made him squirm.

Nope. He'd never get away with it. First off, his

mother would want to know where he'd been and why he was gone so long. All those things that mothers want to know. And if, by some miracle, that didn't happen, surely nosy ole Althea would find out somehow, like she found out every little thing that happened in Foley.

Randall folded the map up and stuffed it into his shirt pocket. He was going to have to think about this one for a while.

*** *** ***

Preacher Ron nodded toward Inez Dawson. "Inez, you want to give us the Sunday school report?"

Inez stood up and faced the congregation. She looked down at her clipboard and cleared her throat.

"There were forty-two children in Sunday school last week," she said, pausing while a few people clapped. "However," she continued, "there were only thirty-one Bibles brought to Sunday school last week." She lowered her head and peered over her glasses at some of the children scattered around the room.

Then she reminded everyone about junior choir practice and sat down.

Randall used a blue colored pencil to fill in the eyes of the little boys and girls on the cover of the church bulletin. The curly-headed children laughed and danced in a field of daisies. A fluffy baby lamb trailed along behind them.

Mickey Ross gave the church treasurer's report.

$22.40 collected in Sunday school. $632.48 collected in tithes and offerings.

Randall colored the center of each daisy bright yellow. Church seemed to get longer every week. And without Jaybird, it wasn't even fun going to the Fellowship Hall afterward. Usually he just grabbed a cupcake and went out back to watch the other kids play tag.

"And now please join me in singing hymn number 38, 'Standing on the Solid Rock,' " Preacher Ron said.

Randall stood up and rested the hymnal on the back of the pew in front of him. He moved his mouth, pretending to sing. His head was too littered up with other stuff to be thinking about singing.

If he didn't do something soon, Queenie was going to tell somebody about Lavonia Shirley and the box. Maybe nobody would believe her, since she talked so crazy. But maybe somebody would. And maybe that somebody would tell somebody, and on and on the news would go, spreading through Foley like wildfire. And everyone would know Queenie had been wandering at night, and would make Mr. Avery send her away.

And even if that didn't happen, the foster care folks from up in Spartanburg were liable to come to Foley and take Moses away because of all the fussing and fighting going on. Leastways, that's what everybody was gossiping about.

There was no doubt about it. He couldn't wait any

longer. He had to talk to Lavonia Shirley and tell her to come get her baby. That's all there was to it. But how?

Then, as if his thoughts had made their way through all that hymn singing and floated skyward, a miracle happened. Randall looked out the window of the Rock of Ages Baptist Church and there was Lavonia Shirley, sitting on the curb in her floppy straw hat.

Randall felt like somebody had flipped the switch of the world to "off." Everything stopped. The singing all around him. His father's feet shuffling on the wooden floor. The old man coughing in the back of the church. Seemed like even his own heartbeat had stopped.

Then he felt himself lean toward his mother. Heard himself whisper, "I'll be right back."

The next thing he knew, he was outside squinting in the bright sun. Organ music drifted out of the windows and swirled around in the still summer air.

Randall looked across the street. The curb was empty. Lavonia was gone.

He shielded his eyes from the glaring sun and searched the empty lot across from the church. Nothing. He raced to the corner and around the Elks Lodge. Then he spotted her, hurrying up the sidewalk away from town. She hiked her flowered skirt up above her knees with one hand and clutched her straw hat with the other.

Randall ran after her. The slap of his sneakers

echoed down the empty street. Lavonia glanced over her shoulder, walking faster. Just as Randall was about to catch up to her, she whirled around to face him.

"What you want?" she said, glaring at Randall. Her voice was hoarse and raspy. She kept one hand on her hat.

Randall was surprised how young she looked. Her bushy black hair seemed to struggle to escape from under the hat. Big looped earrings dangled to her shoulders and glistened in the sun. Her skin was dark and smooth, and her eyes were a peculiar color. Almost gold.

Now that Randall had caught up to her, he felt foolish. He must have been crazy to run after her like this.

He looked down at the sidewalk, wishing the words he should say to her would be written there.

She took her hand off her hat and peered down at Randall. "I *said*, what do you want?"

"I know you're the one who left Moses at the church." Randall kept his eyes down, afraid to look up at Lavonia.

She let out a small breath, like a sigh, and was silent.

Randall looked up. She was studying him through narrowed eyes. She put her hands on her waist. Her arms were long and thin. Her sharp, pointy elbows formed perfect "V"s.

"I don't know Moses," she said in that raspy voice.

"He's a baby," Randall said. "The baby in the box."

Lavonia's arms dropped limply to her sides, and her shoulders drooped slightly, but she kept her gaze on Randall. He wondered if she was thinking about lying to him. Maybe she would say it wasn't her. That he must have her mixed up with somebody else.

"You're right," she said. "It was me."

"Oh." Randall's mind went blank. What was he supposed to say? Why had he done this, anyway?

"What do you want from me?" Lavonia said. Her voice had a sadness to it that made Randall feel bad. He wished he could turn around and go home. But he couldn't. Not now. The cat was already out of the bag. He couldn't put it back.

"Everybody's fighting over him," Randall said.

Lavonia paused for a minute. She kept those gold-colored eyes of hers on him, and he felt himself blush.

"The whole town is all stirred up and taking sides," he said. "Some folks think Miss Frieda ought to take care of him, and some folks think Mrs. Charlotte Jennings ought to. And now the Gilleys don't even come to church anymore." He paused for a minute, but when he saw she wasn't going to say anything, he went on, "Queenie Avery saw you, too. And she keeps talking about you and she's even gone looking for you, and Mr. Avery is scared somebody will put her away in a home. And those foster care people up in Spartanburg are going to come and take Moses away."

There. What else could he say?

Randall studied Lavonia's face. Slowly, slowly, slowly, it softened. She lifted her head slightly and gazed up at the sky. Then she looked at Randall again and said, "His name ain't Moses."

"Oh."

"His name is Nathan."

"Nathan?"

Lavonia nodded. She took her straw hat off. Her wild hair sprang up high on top of her head. Then she pulled her skirt up over her knees and sat down right there on the sidewalk.

Randall sat across from her, waiting.

She shook her head slowly. "I just didn't think I could take care of another baby," she said.

Randall waited.

"Every day I'd open my eyes and feel such a dark heavy thing over me," she went on. "And all my kids needing me. Just needing me all the time."

She fingered the brim of her hat. She had rings on every finger. Rings with colored stones and rings with tiny pearls and plain silver rings.

"How many kids do you have?" Randall said.

She chuckled. "Seems like a hundred sometimes." She twisted a ring around and around on her finger. "Nathan makes six," she said.

Her shoulders lifted as she took a deep breath. She let it out with a whoosh that blew her hair off her forehead. "Six kids and no man," she added.

"Oh."

"I moved in with my cousin Rozene, but that's not working out so good." She put her hat back on and tried to tuck her hair up under it, but little spirals of curls kept springing back out. "Rozene's got her own kids to take care of and all," she went on. "I was trying to find me a job, but what could I do with Nathan?"

She lifted her eyes to look at Randall.

"Uh . . ." Randall tried to think of a good answer, but before he could, Lavonia continued.

"Rozene said her diaper days are over. So there I was. Way out there in that house with all them kids and all and . . ."

She looked up at the sky and shook her head.

"I told Rozene and my kids and everybody that Nathan was with his daddy's people."

She looked at Randall. "I just keep making mistakes," she said. "You ever make mistakes?"

"Sure," Randall said. "All the time."

"I never should have left that child like that," she said. "I knew it the minute I did it, but my old sorry self just did it anyways."

Okay, Randall thought, now is the time.

"You've got to go get him," he said.

Lavonia nodded. "I know. But now I'm scared to."

"How come?"

"What if they put me in jail?" she said. "Ain't you ever heard of child abandonment? That's what I done. Abandonment."

"Aw, nobody'd put you in jail. Not if you go back and get him." Randall tried to make his voice sound sure and confident, but actually he wasn't so sure. What if they *did* put her in jail? What would happen to Moses then? And all those other kids of hers, what about them? Randall was starting to think he hadn't done the right thing after all.

"What's your name?" Lavonia said.

"Randall Mackey."

"Randall Mackey," she repeated, twirling a ring around on one of her long fingers. "Who would've thought I'd need a little ole boy like you to shake me up?"

"I didn't mean to shake you up," Randall said. "I was just trying to do the right thing."

Lavonia reached out and put a hand on Randall's

knee. Her touch was warm. It made Randall's swirling-around insides settle down to an easy calm.

"Then I reckon I got to do the right thing, too, huh?" she said.

Randall nodded.

"Okay, I will." She pushed a tuft of hair out of her eyes. "I got to go home and see to things first," she said. "And then I'll come get my Nathan."

"Okay." Randall felt himself grin. This was good, he thought. This was the right thing.

"I been watching him, you know," she said.

"I know."

"I seen how that church lady's been taking care of him."

"Mrs. Charlotte Jennings," Randall said. "She's Preacher Ron's wife."

He wiped dirt off his Sunday school trousers. "She doesn't have any kids," he added.

Lavonia's face went soft; then she stood up and smoothed her skirt.

"Goodbye, Randall." She wiggled her fingers with all those rings. Then she turned and started off up the sidewalk away from him.

"Lavonia," he called.

She turned.

"How come you left Nathan at the Rock of Ages Baptist Church?"

She shrugged. "First place I come to, that's all," she said.

Randall watched her walk away, her long, skinny legs taking big, silent strides.

Then he turned and ran back toward church, feeling good about his grits and gumption.

15

We have been blessed with a visitor today," Preacher Ron said, "And we hope our visitor gets a blessing from us."

Most everyone tried to act like they weren't staring at Lavonia Shirley, but most everyone was.

Randall's whole body felt like one big twitch. From the minute Lavonia had walked into church, he had felt like he was going to bust wide open. He tried to make his face look curious like everybody else's, like he didn't know why in the world Lavonia Shirley would be showing up out of nowhere like this.

Every now and then he glanced back at her. She wore a long, flowing robe with layers and layers of silky cloth. A yellow-and-orange turban covered up her bushy hair. Randall had never seen anyone in Foley dress like that. She looked like someone right out of a storybook. Like an African queen, or something. It was for certain she didn't look like anybody else sitting there in the Rock of Ages Baptist Church.

"We're just down-home folks," Preacher Ron went on, "raised on corn bread and chicken. And we welcome ALL who choose to join us in this blessed place of brotherhood and worship."

A few people called out, "Amen."

Randall sat on his hands and thunked his heels against the pew until his mother squeezed his knee to make him stop. How was he ever going to sit still through the whole service? What was Lavonia going to do? Was she going to jump up and say she was the one who left Moses on the front steps of this church?

Suddenly a thought popped into Randall's head. What if Lavonia said "Hey" to him? What if she said, "Why, hey there, Randall Mackey"? Or worse yet, what if she told everybody about him chasing after her and all? What if she said, "Randall's the one who saw me leave my baby on the steps of this church"?

Randall couldn't believe he hadn't thought of that before. Why hadn't he told Lavonia that all this mess he'd gotten himself in with Moses was a secret? Why hadn't he explained to her about Queenie and why he couldn't tell anyone why he was outside the church that night?

It was too late now. But at least the few times he had

glanced back there at Lavonia, she hadn't even looked his way.

Preacher Ron kept yelling out words:

LOVE more!

GIVE more!

DO more!

"Don't just take up SPACE," he hollered, pounding his fists on the pulpit. "Make IMPROVEMENTS in this world."

People held up their hands and nodded their heads and called out, "Yes, brother."

When the service was over, folks began wandering over to the Fellowship Hall. Randall watched Lavonia out of the corner of his eye. Her silky robe fluttered in the breeze as she walked along the sidewalk connecting the church to the Fellowship Hall. Her bracelets made tinkling noises with every step. She looked straight ahead, not stopping to speak to anyone along the way. When she came nearer to Randall, her gold-colored eyes flicked in his direction, then, just as quickly, flicked away.

Randall followed her into the Fellowship Hall. By the time he got inside, she was crossing the room toward a cluster of women on the other side. At first the room was buzzing with chatter. Then, slowly, a hushed silence settled in.

When the women in the group across the room realized Lavonia was heading for them, they nervously patted their hair and cleared their throats. Mrs. Charlotte Jennings jostled Moses on her hip and set a smile on her face.

Lavonia stopped in front of Mrs. Jennings and nodded her head toward Moses.

"That's my child," she said.

Moses let out a squeal.

Mrs. Jennings's mouth twitched and she shifted him to the other hip. "I beg your pardon?" she said.

"That's my Nathan."

"Nathan?" Mrs. Jennings chuckled nervously and looked at the women around her.

Lavonia nodded. She reached for the baby. The flowing sleeves of her robe fell away, revealing more bracelets than Randall had ever seen on one person. Shiny silver bracelets stacked clear up to her elbows.

"I'm afraid I don't know you," Mrs. Jennings said. She took a step backward and held Moses against her with both arms.

"I'm Lavonia Shirley."

"Lavonia Shirley?" Mrs. Jennings narrowed her eyes and cocked her head. "Well now, I think maybe I do remember you. I haven't seen you around town in a long time. I thought you moved away."

"I didn't."

"Still, I don't really *know* you," Mrs. Jennings went on. "I can't be giving this baby up to just anybody. Pardon me for casting doubt on you, Mrs. Shirley, but how am I supposed to know he is really your child?"

Some of the women nodded. Moses waved his chubby arms and squealed again.

Lavonia lowered her hands and lifted her chin. "That baby was left in a cardboard box on the steps of this church on the evening of June 15. The box came from behind the Winn-Dixie. It had 'Nabisco Saltine Crackers' written on the side in red. He was wrapped in a yellow-and-white-striped blanket. Three extra T-shirts were tucked in there. Plain white. He wore socks with kittens on them. There was a note written on blue paper with a sunflower at the top. The note said, 'Please take care of me.' I meant to put some apple juice in there, too, but I forgot." Lavonia took a deep breath. "He loves apple juice," she added.

No one moved. No one spoke. Randall watched Lavonia's face, so calm and peaceful. If she really had been scared like she had told him she was, then she must have wrestled that scared feeling and won.

Now it seemed like all eyes in the room shifted from Lavonia to Mrs. Jennings.

Mrs. Jennings kept the smile frozen on her face. Her white neck was flushed and blotchy. And in that brief minute, Randall could tell she had built a wall between herself and Lavonia. Not a wall you could see or touch, but a wall that was solid with bad feelings.

And then Lavonia said, "I want to thank you folks for taking care of my child. You gave me the help I needed to pick myself up and carry on." Lavonia stood straight and tall. She glanced around her at the crowd that had gathered there in the Fellowship Hall. Then she looked at Mrs. Jennings and said, "This is a fine church, and you are fine people."

Mrs. Jennings's face began to change. Slowly, slowly, slowly. The hard edges softened. The tight line of her mouth relaxed. There was no doubt about it, Randall thought. That wall was beginning to crumble.

Lavonia stood there in the middle of all those silent, staring church folks and smiled at Mrs. Jennings.

"I been watching you," she said. "Seeing all you done for my Nathan."

Moses made a cooing sound and patted Mrs. Jennings's face. Lavonia nodded toward the baby that Mrs. Jennings clutched with both arms.

"Looks like you take to babies like a snake to a woodpile," she said.

Mrs. Jennings blushed. The corners of her mouth began to twitch into a smile.

"You've been a good mama to him," Lavonia said.

Crash. That wall came tumbling down.

16

Randall turned to look at the clock on the wall in the back of the church. He could hardly believe only four minutes had gone by since the last time he had checked. How could an hour take so long? It seemed like he'd been in church forever.

Randall slid farther down on the hard church pew. He sure was missing Jaybird. And not just in church. The Gilleys had gone to visit Jaybird's cousins down in Georgia. They'd been gone over a week now, leaving Randall to sit under the porch all by himself, day after day.

Mrs. Mackey poked Randall with her elbow and whispered, "Sit up."

Randall sat up and stared glumly at the pulpit, where Preacher Ron held the collection plate out with both hands.

"We've got to open more than our hearts," he was saying. "We've got to open our wallets."

He handed the collection plate to Wayne Chumley.

"Wayne is coming around to collect money for the Shirley family because they are in NEED."

Randall jumped. He'd been coming to this church his whole life but he still couldn't guess which word Preacher Ron was going to holler.

"They are in NEED of our love," Preacher Ron went on. "They are in NEED of our faith. And they are in NEED of our dollars."

Folks nodded and reached into their pockets and purses.

Preacher Ron wiped his face with a handkerchief. "Those little ole Shirley children and their mama are sheep in the same flock as the rest of us," he said. "And we must not let them DROWN in a sea of troubles."

"No, sir," someone called out.

"That's right," called another.

"We are the little church with the big heart." Preacher Ron clutched a Bible to his chest. "And we MUST not forget it."

"Amen."

"Before we join our voices in song," he said, "Charlotte has an announcement."

Mrs. Jennings stood up and faced the congregation.

"After the service," she said, "the Wednesday night Partners in Prayer group will be meeting in the choir room to discuss the current situation with Moses—I mean, Nathan."

Randall jerked to attention. What did *that* mean? What current situation? Nathan was back home with Lavonia, and everything could just get on back to the way it was before. Why did anybody have to go and discuss stuff?

After church, Randall tiptoed downstairs and stood outside the choir room. The door was closed, but bits and pieces of muffled voices drifted out into the hall.

". . . those children . . ."

". . . this church . . ."

". . . I think . . ."

". . . they said . . ."

Randall pressed his ear against the door and tried to hear all the words instead of just pieces that didn't fit together. But it was no use.

Before long, the sound of metal chairs scraping the linoleum floor made Randall dash back up the stairs just as folks came filing out of the choir room.

Randall raced over to the Gilleys' and scrambled up under the porch. He could hardly wait to tell Jaybird everything he'd missed while he'd been away. Jaybird was waiting for him. He put a finger to his lips and said, "Shhhhh." He pointed to the floor of the porch above them. "Althea's up there," he whispered.

"I heard you!" Althea yelled. She poked a stick through the cracks and jabbed it up and down, up and down.

Randall jerked back out of the way, but Jaybird grabbed the stick and yanked, breaking it with a snap.

"Mama-a-a-a-a," Althea whined.

The screen door slammed above them. Randall and Jaybird laughed. Then Randall told Jaybird everything. He told him about how Lavonia had finally taken Nathan home, and how the ladies from church had sat up nearly all night with Charlotte Jennings 'cause she was so pitiful without that baby. Then he told Jaybird about how those people from social services up in Spartanburg had come down and called on Lavonia and how they said they had concerns.

"What you mean, 'concerns'?" Jaybird asked.

Randall told him what all the church ladies were saying. That Lavonia needed some help being a mama, or else those social services folks might take Nathan away.

"No way," Jaybird had said.

So Randall went on to tell him about how Mrs. Jennings had gotten an idea.

"What idea?" Jaybird said.

"To have a Play and Pray Group."

"What's that?"

"A group where mamas can bring their kids to play while they talk and pray and stuff with the other mamas," Randall said.

"Oh."

"And then Lavonia can come and bring all her kids and the church ladies can help her take care of them."

Althea's face appeared outside the lattice of the fort. "But *I'm* the one who helps with Moses," she said.

"Hush up," Jaybird said, jabbing the broken stick through the lattice. "You ain't even going to that church no more."

Before Althea could start hollering, Randall hurried to tell Jaybird the rest. About how Lavonia didn't seem too interested in coming to the Play and Pray Group, even when the welcoming committee kept calling on her. And how all the ladies couldn't figure out what to do.

"And *then*," Randall went on, "they decided Miss Frieda was the one to do it."

"Do what?"

"Talk some sense into Lavonia."

"Sense about what?"

"About coming to the Play and Pray Group and bringing her kids and all." Randall stopped to catch his breath.

Althea poked her head inside the fort. "Then what happened?" she said, before ducking back out.

"I heard Mrs. Jennings is going over to Miss Frieda's today," Randall said.

"Naw!" Jaybird slapped his knee and shook his head.

"Let's go." Randall scrambled out from under the porch and took off running toward Miss Frieda's. He could hear Jaybird's bare feet slapping the sidewalk behind him.

When they got there, T.J. was throwing a tennis ball against the side of the house.

Miss Frieda stuck her head out of the window and hollered, "Stop that racket, boy!", then ducked back inside.

T.J. grinned at Randall and Jaybird.

"That church lady's in there," he said.

Randall looked toward the house. "What's she saying?"

T.J. shrugged and bounced the ball in the dirt, sending up puffs of dust.

Randall crouched beneath the open window and motioned for T.J. and Jaybird to join him.

Just then Althea came bursting around the corner. Jaybird grabbed her arm and yanked her over beside him.

"Be quiet or go home," he whispered.

She made a face, but she kept quiet. They all

grinned at each other and looked up at the open window above them.

"... seems reluctant to come to our Play and Pray Group," Mrs. Jennings was saying.

Miss Frieda didn't say anything.

Mrs. Jennings went on, "So I've been praying and asking for guidance." She paused. "To help me know what to do," she said.

Miss Frieda just went "Mmmmm."

"And that's why I'm here," Mrs. Jennings said. " 'Cause I see how you take care of these children, and I know you understand what Lavonia is going through." She paused, but when Miss Frieda didn't say anything, she continued. "And I know in my heart that *you* are the person who can help."

"Help do what?" Miss Frieda said.

There was silence for a minute and Randall could hardly keep himself from peeking in the window to see what was going on.

"We were hoping you could convince Lavonia Shirley to come to our Play and Pray Group," Mrs. Jennings said. "So we can help her with the baby and all," she added.

Again there was silence.

"I know we've had our differences in the past, Frieda," Mrs. Jennings said. "But I know that when it's all said and done, well, we both want the same thing."

117

"And what is that, Charlotte?"

"To help Lavonia and those children."

Randall, Jaybird, T.J., and Althea all huddled together beneath the window, waiting. Althea started to giggle and Jaybird clamped his hand over her mouth. They could hear Miss Frieda's heavy breathing. Heard her grunt as she stood up. Her heavy footsteps across the floor.

"I reckon she *could* use some help," Miss Frieda said.

"Then you'll speak to her?"

There was silence. Randall figured Miss Frieda must have nodded her head yes, 'cause Mrs. Jennings said, "I *told* Preacher Ron you would help us."

"But I ain't making no promises," Miss Frieda said.

The screen door squeaked and then slammed shut. The children flattened themselves against the side of the house as the two women went down the front steps to the red-dirt yard.

"Thank you, Frieda," Mrs. Jennings said.

Randall watched her head off down the sidewalk toward the church.

Suddenly Miss Frieda's voice boomed down at them from the porch.

"Tyrone Jamal! Get your sorry self on in here right now!" she hollered. "And tell them other young-uns to go on home."

17

*P*uh-leeeeze, Mama," Althea whined.

The screen door slammed, and Althea stomped on the porch floor, making the boards over Randall and Jaybird rattle.

"Don't argue with me, Althea," Mrs. Gilley called from inside.

"Please, please, please." Althea stamped her foot with each "please."

"Come on," Randall said, motioning to Jaybird. "Let's go see what's going on."

He crawled out from under the porch and brushed the dirt off his knees.

"Mrs. Jennings said I could, Mama," Althea hollered through the screen door. "*Please.*"

But Mrs. Gilley didn't answer. Althea marched down the porch steps.

"What you whinin' about?" Jaybird said, crawling out from under the porch.

Althea crossed her arms and sat on the bottom step. Her lower lip quivered and she swiped at a tear, leaving a streak of dirt across her cheek.

"Mama is so mean," she said.

"How come?" Randall said.

"Lavonia Shirley is going to the Play and Pray Group, and Mama won't let me go."

Althea picked the peeling paint from the banister along the steps.

"*I'm* the one who's supposed to take care of Moses," she said.

"His name is Nathan," Randall said.

"Well, I'm calling him Moses."

"But that ain't his name, dog breath," Jaybird said.

Althea glared at him. "So what?"

Randall watched Althea peel the paint and flick it into the shrubbery.

"Why won't your mama let you go?" Randall asked.

" 'Cause she's mean."

"You better hush up," Jaybird said, glancing toward the open front door.

"She said we don't go to that church no more." Althea flicked a chip of paint at Jaybird. " 'Cause everybody said Miss Frieda was a troublemaker," she added.

"I bet if Mrs. Jennings talked to Mama, she'd

change her mind and then we could come back to church," Jaybird said.

Randall shrugged. "Maybe."

"Ask her," Jaybird said.

Althea nodded so hard one of her braids flopped over into her face. "Yeah, ask her," she said.

"Ask who what?" Randall said.

"Ask Mrs. Jennings to come over here and talk to Mama."

"Yeah," Althea said, "ask Mrs. Jennings to come over here and talk to Mama."

Jaybird shot her a look.

Randall shook his head. "I don't know."

"She'd do it if *you* asked her," Jaybird said. "She likes you."

"Yeah," Althea said. "She don't like us too much."

Jaybird shot her another look.

"I don't think so," Randall said.

"Come on." Jaybird nudged Randall. "Don't you want us to come back to church?"

"Sure I do," Randall said. "But I don't think Mrs. Jennings will listen to *me*."

Althea jumped up and clasped both hands together. "Please, please, please." She shook her clasped hands in Randall's face.

"Oh, all right," Randall said. "I'll try."

When they got to the church, piano music floated out of the basement window.

"Choir practice," Jaybird said.

"Yeah," Randall said. "Maybe we better come back later."

"No, now!" Althea hollered. Then she softened her face and lowered her voice and said, "Please, Randall."

Jaybird and Althea followed Randall through the back door of the church and down the stairs to the choir room. They tiptoed in and sat on the metal folding chairs along the wall.

"Okay, then," Mrs. Jennings was saying. "We'll sing 'When the Roll Is Called Up Yonder' first and 'He Is Mine' second." She closed her hymnal and gathered sheets of music off the table in front of her. "See y'all Sunday," she said.

As the choir members filed out of the room, Randall stood up.

"Mrs. Jennings?" he said.

She looked up. "Well, hey there, Randall," she said. "What're y'all doing?"

"We came to ask you a favor."

"Oh?"

"Althea wants real bad to be the helper for Moses, uh, I mean, Nathan, at that new play group of yours," Randall said. "And, um, she was wondering, I mean, *we* was wondering, well, Jaybird and Althea, and . . ."

Mrs. Jennings chuckled. "Wondering what, Randall?"

"If you would go over to the Gilleys' and make Mrs. Gilley come back to church," Randall said. " 'Cause Jaybird and Althea really want to."

Mrs. Jennings pressed her lips together. "But does *Mrs. Gilley* want to come back to church?" she said.

Althea ran over. "She does," she said. "I know she does. She hates it over at that other church where we been going. She said them busybodies over there are worse than you."

Jaybird punched Althea in the arm. Mrs. Jennings's face twitched slightly, but she smiled.

"Well now, Althea honey, your mama knows this church opens its doors to everyone." She put the sheet music into a folder. "Even those who have shut the doors of their hearts to *us*," she added.

"She ain't shut no door," Althea said. "She just needs you to lead the way to putting away the wrath."

Althea grinned at Jaybird and Randall. Mrs. Jennings's eyebrows shot up.

"Putting away the wrath?" she said.

"You know, like it says in the Bible," Althea said. " 'Let all bitterness and wrath be put away from you with a mallet.' "

Mrs. Jennings smiled. " 'With *all malice*,' " she said. "That's Ephesians."

Althea nodded. "I know it is. I know all them verses perfectly. I should've won that Bible drill, 'cause Maddie Shadd is so stupid and—ow!" Althea grabbed her arm where Jaybird had punched her again.

Randall stepped forward and said, "I just figured, um, I mean, *we* just figured . . ." He glanced back at Jaybird and Althea. "We just figured that since this is the little church with the big heart and all . . . and . . . um . . ."

Randall watched Mrs. Jennings's face go from hard to soft.

"All right," Mrs. Jennings said. "I'll see what I can do."

Randall and Jaybird made Althea sit at the very edge of the fort.

"You keep one arm and one leg *out* of our fort or else you can't sit here at all," Jaybird said.

Althea nodded. "I will."

Randall motioned for them to be quiet. They sat still, staring up at the porch above them. Mrs. Jennings and Mrs. Gilley were talking.

At first Mrs. Gilley's words had come out quick and sharp.

"Yes?" "I see." "Oh?"

But before long she was sounding like somebody who might give in and say, "Yes, we'd love to come back to the Rock of Ages Baptist Church." When Mrs. Gilley offered Mrs. Jennings some diet cola and Mrs. Jennings said yes, she'd love some, Randall made a thumbs-up sign to Jaybird and Althea.

Finally the two women stood up and Mrs. Jennings said, "See you Sunday, then."

Randall and Jaybird and Althea high-fived each other and Jaybird let Althea move just a few inches farther inside their fort.

18

We're selling candy," Althea said when Miss Frieda came to the door.

"Candy?"

"Yes, ma'am."

Miss Frieda stepped out onto the porch. Two small boys came out after her.

"Y'all get on over there to Earlene's like I told you," Miss Frieda hollered at the boys, jerking her head toward the other side of the duplex.

After the boys had scampered away, Miss Frieda sat in a rickety lawn chair on the porch.

"What y'all selling candy for?" she said.

"For church," Randall said.

Althea sat on the porch beside Miss Frieda and grinned up at her. "For the Rolling Pulpit," she said.

Miss Frieda's eyebrows squeezed together. "Rolling pulpit? What in tarnation is that?"

"It's like a traveling church," Randall said. "So old people and sick people and all can—"

"So people can pretend like they're in church even if they have their pajamas on," Althea said.

"Preacher Ron and the Celebration Choir and everybody can come right to your house," Randall said.

"Only it costs money," Jaybird added. "To use the church bus and all. So the Sunday school is selling candy to help pay for it."

"I thought y'all quit that church," Miss Frieda said to Jaybird.

"Mrs. Jennings came to talk to Mama," Jaybird said.

"Oh, she did?"

"Yeah," Althea said. "And she told her to put away her wrath with a mallet."

Miss Frieda chuckled. "Lawd, you sure can talk some talk, Althea."

Althea grinned. "*And*," she said, "Mrs. Jennings told Mama to be ye forgiving. Do you know what 'ye' means?"

Before Miss Frieda could answer, Althea said, "It means 'you.' That's Bible talk."

Miss Frieda's stomach jiggled as she laughed. "And did your mama be forgiving?" she asked.

Althea shook her head. "Not at first," she said. "At first Mama told her she shouldn't have waited till her crow got cold."

Miss Frieda laughed and slapped her knee.

Althea grinned. "Mama told her she was liable to choke."

Miss Frieda wiped at tears with a balled-up tissue. "Why was she liable to choke?"

" 'Cause the easiest way to eat crow is while it's still warm." Althea beamed at Miss Frieda. "The colder it gets, the harder it is to swallow."

At that, Miss Frieda held her stomach and laughed so hard Randall thought she was going to fall right out of her chair.

Althea had a look of pure delight on her face. "And now we're going back to church, and I get to be the helper for Moses at the Play and Pray Group," she said. "Ain't that nice?"

Miss Frieda settled back in her chair and shook her head. "Lawd, I swear, child, you take the cake." She wiped the back of her neck with the tissue. "Yeah, I reckon that is nice," she added.

Jaybird poked Randall, and Randall said, "We got to get on back to the church. Do you want to buy some candy?"

"Sure, I'll buy one." She put her hands on her hips and narrowed her eyes at Randall. "But I don't want no church rolling into my house," she said.

"No, ma'am."

Miss Frieda went inside and came back with a dollar bill and a brown paper bag.

"Take this over there to that praying group of yours," she said, handing the bag to Randall.

"What is it?"

"Just some old stuff I had around here that's getting in the way. Some baby clothes and a couple of little ole toys."

"Thank you." Randall went down the porch steps and put the bag in the wagon with the boxes of candy bars.

Althea skipped off down the sidewalk. "If you want the Rolling Pulpit to come, just holler," she called over her shoulder.

Miss Frieda flapped her hand at Althea. "Git on outta here," she said.

～～～

When they got to the church, Randall, Jaybird, and Althea took the wagon around back to the Fellowship Hall. Inside, tables had been set up for kids to turn in their money and pick up more candy bars to sell.

"Let me pull the wagon," Althea said.

"No," Jaybird said, pushing her hand away.

"Then let me count the money."

"I already counted it," Randall said. "Eight dollars."

"Then—hey, look!" Althea pointed at a group of

children who had just come into the Fellowship Hall. One of them was carrying a baby. Behind them was Lavonia Shirley.

Lavonia crossed the room, smiling and nodding at some of the church ladies. Her hair was tied back with a silk scarf that floated out behind her as she walked.

Mrs. Jennings looked up from counting money. "Well, hey there, Lavonia," she said.

"I came to help," Lavonia said.

Althea pointed to one of the girls with Lavonia. "She can be on my candy team. What's her name?"

"Miracle," Lavonia said.

"Miracle?" Althea cocked her head. "What kinda name is that?"

Mrs. Jennings put her hand on Althea's shoulder. "Where are your manners, Althea?" she said. "Have you met Mrs. Shirley?"

"I heard about her 'cause of Queenie."

"Queenie Avery?"

Randall's heart dropped clear down to his stomach. They weren't supposed to be talking about Queenie.

"Yes, ma'am," Althea said. "Queenie's all the time talking about Lavonia Shirley."

Randall wanted to jump on Althea. Knock her right down to the floor and cover her mouth.

"Poor ole Queenie." Mrs. Jennings shook her head. "She sure does talk crazy sometimes."

Althea grinned. "She sure does."

"Anyway . . ." Mrs. Jennings put her arm around Althea's shoulder, "Lavonia, this is Althea Gilley."

Randall let his breath out with a whoosh. Maybe they weren't going to talk about Queenie, after all.

"And that there is her brother, Jaybird." Mrs. Jennings nodded at Jaybird.

Lavonia smiled.

"And this is Randall Mackey," Mrs. Jennings said.

Randall watched Lavonia's face as she shifted her gaze from Jaybird to him. She nodded and said, "Pleased to meet you, Randall Mackey."

And then, just ever so slightly, she winked.

■■ ■■ ■■

"We will load up our FAITH and our PRAYERS and ALL of the goodness in our hearts," Preacher Ron was saying. "LOAD it right up onto our Rolling Pulpit and spread it A-A-A-LL over Foley, South Carolina."

All around the church, folks raised their hands and waved their Bibles and called out.

"Hallelujah!"

"Praise be!"

Preacher Ron took his jacket off and loosened his tie. His hair hung in wet clumps on his forehead. "We MUST spread the good works of this church to our friends and neighbors."

Randall watched the preacher wave his Bible in the air. A fan whirred back and forth from a chair beside the pulpit, spreading a cool breeze from one side of the room to the other.

Randall's mother had let him take his jacket off, but his shirt was still damp against his back. Even with all the doors and windows open, the air inside was thick with heat. Randall folded his church bulletin and fanned himself.

"And now, brothers and sisters," Preacher Ron said, "let us lift our voices in celebration and praise of the good works of this church by singing hymn number 27, 'When the Roll Is Called Up Yonder.' "

He nodded toward Norma Jakes at the organ, then motioned for the congregation to stand.

Randall stood between his mother and father and watched the Celebration Choir sway from side to side with the music. Folks began to sing, and soon feet tapped the floor, hands clapped, and heads nodded.

Bucky Farwood stood beside the organ with a microphone and sang out, "Hallelujah."

At first Randall sang soft, like he usually did. But before long the whole room seemed to vibrate with the rhythm of stamping feet and clapping hands, and Randall began to sing louder.

"When the r-o-l-l-l-l is called up yonder . . ."

He tapped his toes and drummed his fingers against

the wooden pew in front of him as the music swirled around the room.

Mrs. Charlotte Jennings stood in front of the choir, waving her arms in time to the music. Her head jerked, making her stiff hairdo quiver from side to side.

Randall looked back at the sixth row on the left. Althea was standing right up on the seat of the pew, lifting her skinny legs clear up to her chin as she marched to the beat. Even Jaybird was singing, wagging his head from side to side, every now and then grinning up at his mother.

Way in the back, Mr. Avery held his cap in his gnarled hands. His eyes were closed and his thin gray hair bounced slightly as he nodded with the music. Randall wondered if maybe he was thinking about Queenie, sitting at home on their old couch, clutching her big red purse.

Beside Mr. Avery, Lavonia Shirley waved one hand gracefully in the air, the sleeve of her silky robe fluttering. Her silver bracelets and shiny rings glittered in the morning sun that streamed through the open windows. She bounced Nathan on her hip. Up and down. Up and down. Her other five children stood shoulder to shoulder beside her.

When the music stopped, everyone clapped and mopped their foreheads and wiped their necks with tissues.

Preacher Ron called out, "I FEEL the love!"

Mrs. Mackey hollered, "That's right."

Someone in the back of the room called out, "I feel it, too!"

Then Preacher Ron leaned over the pulpit and gestured toward the ceiling. "This little ole building of brick and mortar is NOT the Rock of Ages Baptist Church," he said.

Then he threw his arms out wide and hollered, "These PEOPLE are the Rock of Ages Baptist Church."

Randall looked around the room. Everyone was nodding and grinning, and Randall felt himself grinning, too.

Then Preacher Ron pointed to the sign over the organ and said real slow, "We *are* the little church with the big heart."

Shouts of "Amen" filled the room.

Randall looked back once more at Lavonia Shirley. She turned her gold eyes to meet his and smiled. Then she winked that tiny little wink again.

Randall winked back.

Then he looked around him at all those people in that little church, and he called out, "Amen!"

ACKNOWLEDGMENTS

It takes a village to make a book. I would like to thank my village:

My agent, Barbara Markowitz, for being my partner, fan, and friend; my writers' group, for telling it like it is; Nancy the Pool Girl Farrelly, who critiques with honesty, humor, and respect for the Sisterhood; Leslie Guccione, for sharing poignant stories of her beloved mother, Winnie, who inspired the character of Queenie in this novel; Willy and Grady, for loving me and eating leftovers; and, of course, the "village" at Farrar, Straus and Giroux: my brilliant editors, Frances Foster and Janine O'Malley; my charming (and never irritating) copy editor, Elaine Chubb; my talented designer, Barbara Grzeslo, and my productive production manager, Daniel Myers; and, lastly, thank you to the good Baptists of the South, whose kindness and unwavering faith inspired my life, as well as this story.